Summer stood above him like a mythical deity in the pale, rain-washed light. Her towel was draped loosely over her curves and as he watched, she let it slip down, slowly, tantalizingly, then drop away. Entranced, he stood very still, watching her every move. The shadows of raindrops on the windowpane rippled across her body in a hypnotic dance. He swallowed hard as she stepped toward him.

"Summer, I—" He held out the sweatshirt, and she took it away from him, tossing it on the bed with a strange beckoning smile on her lips.

"Don't say a word, Ryan." She kissed him, her naked body moving enticingly against his, silky smooth and scalding.

Her damp hair smelled of shampoo, and he buried his face in it, not wanting to think, knowing he had to, he had to keep his senses in check. "Summer . . . Summer. What are you doing?"

"You have to ask?" she mumbled.

He cupped her face in his hands and tilted it up to him, his mind spinning as he fell into her smoldering emerald gaze. He had to make her stop, before it was too late. "Summer, this is . . . You need to—"

"Touch you," she said.

WHAT ARE *LOVESWEPT* ROMANCES?

They are stories of true romance and touching emotion. We believe those two very important ingredients are constants in our highly sensual and very believable stories in the LOVE-SWEPT line. Our goal is to give you, the reader, stories of consistently high quality that may sometimes make you laugh, sometimes make you cry, but are always fresh and creative and contain many delightful surprises within their pages.

Most romance fans read an enormous number of books. Those they truly love, they keep. Others may be traded with friends and soon forgotten. We hope that each LOVE-SWEPT romance will be a treasure—a "keeper." We will always try to publish

LOVE STORIES YOU'LL NEVER FORGET BY AUTHORS YOU'LL ALWAYS REMEMBER

The Editors

Loveswept ®745

INTO THE STORM

RILEY MORSE

BANTAM BOOKS
NEW YORK · TORONTO · LONDON · SYDNEY · AUCKLAND

INTO THE STORM

A Bantam Book / June 1995

ISBN 0-553-44509-X

Published simultaneously in the United States and Canada

PRINTED IN THE UNITED STATES OF AMERICA

OPM   0 9 8 7 6 5 4 3 2 1

ONE

"I don't want any tricks from you, Ryan."

"Tricks? Me? You don't think that I—"

"Yes, I do. Why can't you behave like a professional member of this staff for once?"

Ryan Jericho took a long, slow breath trying to calm down. "You said the proposal was going before the board of directors next month."

"It was," said Roscoe Williams, placing both chubby hands on his desk and leaning forward. "But we scheduled a special session for this morning. The Humantec representatives were kind enough to come all the way from Atlanta to give us a demonstration today."

"How nice."

"Now, Ryan, I advise you to—"

"To what? Sit still while you squander the clinic's money on high-tech toys?" Ryan clenched his teeth, holding back the brunt of his anger. He'd left town for five days and look what happened. The job interview had gone well, but if the research team did hire him, what was going to happen here when he left for good? He had to be certain the halfway house was set up before his time ran out.

Roscoe peered stonily over the top of his glasses. "Sandy Flats Mental Health Clinic needs a state-of-the-art computer system."

Ryan stood up slowly, all six feet three inches of him unfolding to tower over the clinic's administrator. "Says who? Some slick sales rep from Humantec Software? C'mon, Ros, you ought to know how those guys operate by now. We don't need half of what they're trying to sell us."

"That's not your decision."

"And what about funding for the halfway house?"

"We can't do everything for everybody, Ryan."

"But—"

"And we can't pass up this opportunity—"

"No halfway house? What about those kids? You can't do it, Ros."

Roscoe shoved a pamphlet across his desk toward Ryan. "This is a description of Humantec's system. It's quite impressive. I recommend you take a look at it."

Ryan gave a snort. "No thanks."

"There's nothing you can do now, Ryan—except cause trouble." Roscoe's bushy gray eyebrows lifted in unison. "And you wouldn't do that. Would you?"

Ryan tossed the document up and caught it. "C'mon, Ros, have I ever—?"

"Yes."

"Well then, I suppose you know what to expect."

Ryan's temper was simmering just below boil as he wound through the clinic's maze of halls toward his office. He'd let them know about trouble . . . just as soon as he figured out the best way to make it. Someone must be doing a real slick sales job.

It was a long shot, a real long shot, but if he had the right kind of ammunition, he knew he could fight this thing. Hell, he had to try.

What he needed was information. And a plan—that would help of course.

By the time he rounded the corner, his brain was racing at as fast a clip as his feet. He saw, but ignored, the mop and bucket propped against the wall and the bright shine of newly waxed linoleum. Without warning, his feet shot out in front of him and in the next instant he was careening across the slick floor, his tennis shoes where his head should've been.

He slid with the deadly accuracy of a tracking missile straight at the woman walking down the hall. If she'd been the only person within twenty miles, he couldn't have missed her. He was having that kind of day.

His right leg hooked both of hers, and they fell in an ungraceful tangle, coasting into a nearby table with a loud thud. The large gardenia-filled vase sitting on top teetered precariously for a moment and then fell. She reached up and caught it, but not before the water poured out.

"Nice save," he said. "Almost."

Through the dripping curtain of blond hair plastered across her impish face, she gave him a look that could have killed if she hadn't looked so ridiculous with that gardenia blossom on top of her head.

Ryan snickered, and the snicker turned into a chuckle. He shook his head, trying to regain enough control to apologize. It must have been the sheer sense of release the humor brought, but when he looked at her again, his efforts deteriorated into full-blown laughter.

She blinked, and her expression changed completely. A pair of huge emerald-green eyes were now staring at him as if he'd sprouted horns. "I . . . I'm so sorry—" she said, trying to wiggle away from him.

"My fault," he said, gasping for breath.

"Oh no, really. I apologize." Her voice was high and tight.

"I plowed into you . . . remember?" He calmed down just enough to smile for a moment, but she was too busy trying to untangle her legs from his without letting her straight skirt inch up any higher. "Ah yes, waxed linoleum," he said affably. "It'll do it every time." He leaned back on his elbows to observe her.

"Every time? Oh . . . yes. Of course." She grabbed the red leather briefcase that had landed next to her and pulled it onto her lap. A protective move if he ever saw one. He really should try to explain. And there was that look again. She was definitely frightened, but trying hard to cover it. He reached forward to pull her ankle out from under his knee. At his touch she jerked her leg away and struggled quickly to her feet. Jabbering something about finding a nurse, she backed up a few steps, watching him warily, then turned and half ran down the hall.

A nurse? He didn't need a nurse. He wasn't hurt. He shook his head. She's cute, he thought, but definitely strange. Too bad. She was about the best thing that had happened to him all day. Slowly, he picked up the pamphlet he'd dropped during the fall. It was wet.

A good sign, he thought, holding one away from him to drip on the floor.

"Ryan, did you see the Humantec rep come through here, she—Good Lord, what happened?"

"Not a thing, Ros, just relaxing."

Roscoe looked at him skeptically and then shrugged as if he didn't even want to ask. "Well, please relax someplace else, you look like one of the patients."

"I do?" Ryan looked down at his T-shirt and worn jeans, and chuckled. "So that's why she was so upset—"

"What?"

"Oh . . . nothing, nothing at all."

"Where were you, Summer? We've got to get on the road if I'm going to get to Atlanta in time to catch my plane."

"You wouldn't believe me if I told you." Summer Keeton shivered as she watched her business partner, Maxwell Pelion, struggle with the decrepit van's gear shift. "Jiggle it up to the right and then back to reverse," she said. "That's it. Let's get out of here."

"Now you're talking. I thought you were just going to tidy up. Looks like you decided on a full shower."

"Very funny," she said, twisting her damp curls into a bun.

"What happened in there? I've been waiting twenty minutes."

"I was . . . delayed." No way was she going to tell Max she'd just been attacked by a psychotic—a huge shaggy-haired man with the wildest eyes she'd ever seen. "That was a red light you just ran, Max."

"Yellow."

"Red." Okay, so maybe the man wasn't psychotic. She couldn't tell, she wasn't a doctor. But she definitely wouldn't want to meet up with him again. He wasn't normal, that much was certain. Despite the heat of the South Carolina spring, another shiver ran down her spine.

"Well kid, I believe we just sold another system," said Max, chuckling as he pulled out onto the highway.

"We did it?"

"Yep. Your brainchild is gonna make us rich. Quite a team, aren't we?"

"I suppose," she answered distractedly.

"What is it, Summer? I thought you'd be every bit as happy as I am."

She stared out of the window.

"Loosen up," he said after a moment. "Your hard work is finally paying off, kid. This is the easy part. Just remember, all you have to worry about are your computers."

She leaned her head back and closed her eyes. If that were only true, she thought. Humantec Software was a success. Her system was selling. So why did she feel like her life was tilting out of control?

Five weeks later, Summer stood in the parking lot of Sandy Flats Mental Health Clinic, worrying about everything but her computers.

"And one more thing, Summer," Max said, leaning from the window of his newly acquired Fiat and grinning up at her. "I encountered a slight problem."

Summer's stomach tightened as she squinted at Max in the hot morning sun. "So that's why you're leaving."

Max shook his head. "No, not at all. The deal in Bombay could really come through. We've got a chance to go international. I've gotta get over there, you know how it is."

"Yes, I know." She took a deep breath and would have counted to ten if she wasn't afraid he'd take off before she'd reached three. "What's the problem, Max?" She ignored his broad grin. "You're not leaving me with a mess again, are you?" She knew she should have come down with him yesterday. Max tended to get a little enthusiastic with his promises when she wasn't around. But she'd stayed an extra day in Atlanta working on the system enhancements he'd promised on his last trip. She couldn't let him get away without some answers.

"Is this nice, shiny finish scratch resistant?" she asked, as she ran her hand along the Fiat's gleaming red fender.

"Careful, Summer."

She gave him a meaningful look.

"It's nothing you can't handle. Just the usual last-minute fuss because someone's money got diverted to fund our project. Now c'mon—"

"What did you promise them this time?"

"Summer, relax for once. All you have to worry about—"

"—Are the computers. Yes, I know. But—"

"Settle down. Roscoe backs us completely. He'll keep the guy out of your hair."

She leaned against the fender and could almost hear him wince. "Who's Roscoe?"

"Roscoe Williams, the clinic's administrator."

"And who's he supposed to keep out of my hair?"

Max put his hands over his face in exasperation. "Try to enjoy yourself, Summer. You deserve it. Just do what you do best, set up the system and everything else will fall into place."

"And if it doesn't?"

"What's the matter? Afraid you can't handle it?"

Her back straightened automatically. "You know I can," she said, pushing away from the car.

"Don't worry, Summer." His voice softened. "I would never leave you with anything you weren't prepared to take on. You know that, don't you?"

She managed a smile. He was right. He'd always been straight with her. "I guess I'm just a little jumpy around this place," she said. "That's all."

"You'll do fine, kid," said Max as he slowly eased the Fiat away from her. "I promise."

He drove off, stirring up a small cloud of dust in the packed sand of the parking lot. Summer coughed and adjusted the tight bun at the nape of her neck, reclasping the gold barrette as it popped open at her nervous tug. She took a deep breath and turned on her heel to face the white stuccoed building that housed the clinic.

Leaning back in her chair with a practiced casualness, Summer watched Roscoe. He was even more nervous than she was. His gaze stayed fixed on the door of the small auditorium as the last of the staff filed in.

"No, don't believe he'll show," he said, with a small, satisfied smile. "I just gave him a copy of your contract to review. That ought to take him a while to get through."

"Mr. Williams, I'm certain this orientation session

will put everyone at ease," she said in her most sooth-ing tone. "Humantec Software has never had a dissatis-fied customer."

"I don't mean to alarm you, but—" Roscoe lowered his voice to a whisper. "Dr. Jericho isn't a bad sort . . . usually. Best psychologist we have—gifted with the younger clients." One of his eyes twitched behind his glasses as he spoke. "He tends to get very involved with his work—"

"I can understand that." So did she.

"And he had quite extensive plans that were, well, shelved for the moment. He isn't happy."

"I see." Summer smiled up at the puffy face lowered toward her in concern. "Please, you needn't worry about a thing."

"I just wanted to warn you."

"Thanks," she said, her smile still intact.

"Are we ready?" he asked, pulling at his collar.

Summer nodded.

"Folks . . . may I have your attention please . . ."

As Roscoe began his introductory speech, Summer watched the reactions in her audience.

The faces looking back at her were grim.

Be tough. Her father's military bark sounded in her ear.

She tried to pick out a few possible allies in the crowd. There weren't many. This was still a malleable group, she told herself, they hadn't seen her system yet.

"Sandy Flats Mental Health Clinic is pleased to welcome Humantec Software into our family." Ros-coe's voice boomed loudly in the cramped room. He nodded in Summer's direction.

She gave her audience a wide grin.

"With Ms. Summer Keeton's help, computer technology will become an integral part of . . ."

Summer noted the increasingly wary looks as the staff's full attention focused on her. She'd encountered this often enough. Every time Max used his sales tricks. He was a wonderful guy but when it came to business, he played by entirely different rules. Maxwell Pelion the salesman was undeniably ruthless.

He would single out a few key people to get the contract signed as quickly as possible. The papers would all be in order before problems could arise—well before any opposition could organize. Then she would be called in to install the system. His technique worked, but it bothered her just the same. It was a nightmare the first time she'd done it. But she'd learned a few techniques of her own since then. Mainly how to calm the storm Max left her so she could get on with her job.

It wasn't the best way to do business, but Humantec was a success, she couldn't deny that. If she had to work with these people, angry or otherwise, at least she knew it was for her computer system. And it was a good system too. Hadn't it been featured last year in *Health Systems Quarterly*? Her own software. She always had that.

". . . These computers will unlock new worlds . . ." Roscoe proclaimed expansively.

Summer waited, keeping her hands folded loosely in her lap. She tried to look confident and friendly, a feat that was becoming more of a chore the longer Roscoe went on.

A loud creak jarred her concentration as the door at the rear of the auditorium swung open.

"Hello, Ros." The man's soft baritone crossed the room with the impact of a shouted command. "Don't let me interrupt," he said, "not just yet anyway." He stepped in, letting the door slam shut behind him.

Summer's throat went bone-dry as she recognized the tall figure in the dark T-shirt. He stood for a moment at the back of the room against a pale wall that accentuated his broad shoulders and powerful build. There was no mistaking the fierce determination etched deeply into his otherwise handsome face. She tried to swallow but found she couldn't.

The man's strong, even features were carved into a ruggedness that was positively lethal, and his steel-blue gaze was focused entirely on her. She watched motionlessly, her stomach squeezing against her spine as he walked slowly, deliberately to the front of the room.

"Ah . . . hello, Dr. Jericho," said Roscoe. "Nice of you to join us."

What? Summer's breathing skipped out of rhythm for a brief but disconcerting moment. Dr. Jericho?

His faded jeans looked out of place among the business suits around him. So was the thick mane of dark hair that fell raggedly to his shoulders. But from the looks he was getting, he was obviously admired at the clinic.

Picking up an empty chair, Dr. Jericho repositioned it, extending the otherwise full front row out into the aisle. He sat down, looking remarkably like a wild man waiting to attack.

Summer instructed her stomach to relax its grip on her backbone and made herself meet his stare. No, he wasn't crazy. Incredibly, Dr. Jericho seemed very much in possession of himself—and the rest of the room as well.

She wouldn't let him unnerve her. She forced her

gaze to calmly scan the expectant faces of her audience. Their attention was now riveted on Jericho. He was no different from anyone else, she told herself, just another staff member who would need a little extra convincing. Well, maybe a lot of extra convincing.

"And now," said Roscoe, his voice booming, "I would like to present Ms. Summer Keeton. Ms. Keeton will be here for a few weeks to install our new computer system." His gaze flickered to Jericho. "She'll explain our new system in detail, and to your satisfaction, I am sure."

The applause was scattered and died out quickly. Person by person, heads slowly turned and gazes rested speculatively on Summer. Recognizing the carnivorous gleam in the eyes that focused on her, she stood slowly, stiffening her wobbly knees, and met their looks with a steady smile. Deliberately relaxing her pose, she addressed the group, willing competence and geniality into every word.

She'd been harassed before, and knew the warning signals well. They were all flashing now. But no one was going to disrupt her presentation, not even Jericho. Her lecture—normally guaranteed to placate antagonists and absolutely dazzle the moderately interested— had better convince this guy.

Resisting the urge to check her hair, she quelled any movement that might be interpreted as nervousness. He's just a customer to be persuaded, she reminded herself, no different from any other. Max wouldn't blink an eye at him and neither would she.

But the power that flowed around Jericho like an eddying current made every muscle in her body tense.

She barreled through her standard happy-to-be-here spiel.

He was still glaring at her from his prominent seat in the aisle a few long moments later. But she kept smiling as if his look was one of total approval rather than abject condemnation.

Opening the flipchart beside her, she launched into her carefully planned presentation. She described her favorite module—the data base programs, tapping lightly on the red and black system diagram with her metal pointer. The data base she'd designed herself was Humantec's biggest selling point. When she installed the system, she would customize it to meet the specific needs of Sandy Flats clinic.

"Excuse me, Ms. . . . ah . . . Keeton."

Summer's hand tightened around her pointer at the low, liquid tone. "Yes?"

Reluctantly, she turned toward the aisle seat, her gaze immediately caught and held by the most intense eyes she'd ever encountered.

"Ms. Keeton, just who came up with all this?" He motioned toward the chart with one large hand.

"I did, at least the interface that you'll see," she said, oddly gratified that he'd asked the question about her best work. "Humantec's basic package is generic. I like to think of it as a circus tent that covers several acts at the same time. The office automation products would be the acts in each ring and the data base—"

"Oh. I see," he said, his lips curling wickedly. "Now that we've bought the big top, you're telling us the clowns come extra."

A snicker rippled through the group.

"Clowns?" She was holding her pointer in a death grip now. "We do have data base software that—"

"Yes. The clown act."

Loosening her fingers with controlled effort, she allowed his taunt to go unchallenged. She couldn't let this man disrupt her show, but arguing with him would be a big mistake. The staff was obviously sympathetic to Dr. Jericho. Going up against him now would likely push that sympathy into outright support.

"The office automation is standard," she said evenly, "but our custom-designed data bases—"

"The clowns." His smile broadened without softening the ice in his eyes.

"I prefer to think of our data bases as something more along the lines of elephants," she said, smoothing the defensive edge of her response. "They're not absolutely necessary, but they pull a great deal of weight."

She took a breath and pumped out her supporting statistics as if they were water on a fire. As she spoke, she tried to focus on the rest of her audience, being sure to make eye contact with anyone who looked interested, anyone not in the aisle on the front row.

But the impatient shift of a pair of muscular legs molded into tight jeans pulled her eyes there anyway. She stiffened her back. So his presence was unquestionably imposing, she was the one in control.

She began drawing red lines across her diagram, slow and straight, connecting each of the system's modules as she described their purpose.

"Ms. Keeton?"

The baritone wiped her mind clean. For a horrifying instant her next thought hung partially formed in the void. All that came to her was that disturbing blue stare. It was as if she were being sucked into it. She turned toward her flipchart, blinking the familiar lines and boxes of the diagram back into focus before she faced him again.

"These data base, ah . . . elephants . . ." he was saying, "what do they eat?" Surprisingly, his low voice held a trace of humor now.

"Peanuts," she said. Her silk shirt dampened beneath the ivory linen suit as she struggled to gather her thoughts. Peanuts, jeez.

"You've described an interesting package there." He wasn't letting up. "But what I'd like to know is how much extra does it cost to—"

"Humantec is reasonable in its negotiations," she said briskly. "Our package offers not only the best in spreadsheet and word processing software—" she drew bright red circles on the flipchart—"it integrates several data bases from key sources." If Jericho wanted to skirmish, he'd have to find another battleground, this territory was hers.

But he remained silent, arms folded across his chest, lips set in a crooked, half-musing line. The look that had held her mind hostage was turned inward now, dark and unreadable.

She ended her presentation, realizing she had no idea what kind of impression she'd made on her audience. Her orientation was designed to soothe tension and present Humantec at its best. She could only hope it worked.

Half of her senses had functioned, allowing the familiar explanations to come out almost normally, while the other half clung to the strange Dr. Jericho, asking a thousand unanswerable questions. She'd thought he was a maniac. And now? It was nerves. That weird, jittery feeling was just a bad case of nerves, and she was going to get control of it—now.

Summer concentrated on nodding pleasantly at the line of people filing out of the auditorium. When she spotted Jericho leaving, she breathed a heartfelt sigh of relief.

"Well done, Ms. Keeton," said Roscoe, his smile beaming approval. "A brilliant presentation."

"Thank you." She'd pulled it off then. Good. Opening her briefcase, she carefully arranged her notes, dismayed at the way the papers fluttered shakily in her hands.

"I was surprised Ryan Jericho didn't make more trouble. A testament to your powers of persuasion. I know from my own experience he can put some real pressure on."

"Oh?"

"You were lucky," he added.

She resisted the urge to nod heartily in agreement.

"I have to warn you, Ms. Keeton. Just because Ryan Jericho skipped this opportunity to . . . voice his displeasure doesn't mean he's giving up." Roscoe pushed his glasses down and looked over them. "No sir. If he had his way . . . well . . . those boxes of computers down the hall would be shipped back today."

She grinned to keep from chewing her lip. "Our strategy is to get the network up and people using the system right off," she said. "It'll sell itself, and we'll have plenty of support from your staff." She picked up her briefcase. "Humantec will win over Dr. Ryan Jericho. I'm sure of it."

Ryan quickly left the clinic's administration hall, his anger unabated. What had just happened in there? He'd had it all planned. Push the rep from Humantec into deep water right from the start. Let the staff see for themselves what Roscoe had done with their funds. He was going to lead a walkout, make a big show of it —and watch Humantec sink like a rock.

Damn. Keeton should have been easier to handle. She'd looked so young and inexperienced when he'd run into her in the hall that day. Maybe if she hadn't been so cute, he might have been able to pull it off. No, that wasn't fair. The woman had her act together. He'd just have to work on his.

"Ryan, buddy. You leaving?"

Ryan tossed the keys to his Jeep from one hand to the other. "You've gone too far this time, Roscoe. If you think you're going to get away with this fast one, you're wrong."

"You do understand that this is all in the best interests of the clinic," said Roscoe as he pulled a large cotton handkerchief from his pocket.

"The staff should have been consulted. There's no excuse for that." Ryan opened the car door with a frustrated yank.

"You'll get to look at the software firsthand next week," said Roscoe, wiping the handkerchief across his forehead.

Ryan shook his head. It wasn't that he liked causing Roscoe so much trouble. And he hadn't, for most of the eight years he'd worked at the clinic. But ever since Alicia died he'd felt like he was running in the wrong race. He had to get out of it, now. "Ros, just tell that Humantec rep she can leave her computers out of my office. I'm not ready to—"

"Look, we've contracted for everyone to be a part of the system—"

"Part of the system? Each of us an insignificant cog in an overpriced machine. One less cog won't mat—"

Roscoe cleared his throat. "Dr. Ryan Jericho, as long as you're a part of this clinic, you're a part of the system. I mean it. You're getting a computer."

"Oh, all right. Let her put it in if it'll make you happy." He slid onto the sun-warmed seat. "I'll try to keep from smashing it—for a few days at least."

"Listen, Ryan, you really should give Humantec a chance."

"I attended the orientation session, didn't I?"

"Precisely my point." Roscoe sighed loudly and put his hand on top of the Jeep. "Just try to remember Ms. Keeton is here to help us. So no more trouble . . . okay?"

"I'm an honest man, Ros. I can't make any promises along that line." Ryan gave him a pointed stare. Roscoe had never been good at confrontation. A lot of bark but no bite. "I'm taking the afternoon off. If anyone needs me, my answering machine'll be on." That ought to make him happy.

"Ryan, this project is important for the clinic. You understand that, don't you?"

"And the halfway house isn't? I have just one question," he said, shoving on his sunglasses. "Why was the handling of the Humantec project so quick and quiet, Ros?"

"There wasn't time to follow all the usual procedures," said Roscoe, stepping away from the car. "We would have missed out on a great deal."

"What deal?"

"You know I wouldn't have supported Humantec's system if I didn't think—"

"Ros, what is this great deal we got?"

Roscoe folded his handkerchief and put it back in his pocket before answering. "Humantec agreed to install the system in four weeks rather than the usual six. That means, we'll be on-line by the time the commission inspects for accreditation next month."

"And what if the system isn't up by then?" asked Ryan.

"We have the option of canceling the project—or at least the data base module."

"Oh?"

"Not that we would, of course. Don't go getting any ideas now."

"Ideas? Me?"

"I have the utmost confidence in our Ms. Keeton. Yes, Humantec is here to stay."

Somehow Ryan kept from grinning outright. "I think I'll head on out to the swamp," he said. Let Roscoe relax—for now at least, while he considered what to do with this choice bit of news. "Think I might try to get in a few hours of fishing later on this evening."

"Good, good. You take all the time you need," said Roscoe congenially.

He was going to take some time all right, time to study that contract. Hell, he'd even try to dig up the pamphlet describing Humantec's system—the one Roscoe had forced on him weeks ago. It had to be around somewhere. All he needed now was to work out a strategy.

He glanced in the rearview mirror as he pulled out onto the street. Roscoe was still standing in the parking lot with a look of satisfaction spreading across his chubby face. Old Roscoe had been a good friend through this rough year, he hated fighting with him. Humantec was his real target, but if Roscoe, or anybody else got in the way—whether they had gorgeous green eyes or not, they were going to have to tangle with him. He'd make sure of that.

He drove fast as he left town, letting the warm, June air batter his face, soothing him with its senseless persistence. So the morning's meeting hadn't gone as he'd expected. So he'd tried a few shots and then sat there in silence listening to the woman, just like everyone else.

Summer. The name sure didn't fit. She was as wintry as they come with that creamy white skin and icicle glare. He'd planned to intimidate her, but she hadn't even flinched. It was that hard look she'd leveled at him the moment he'd entered the room that got his attention. Something about it intrigued him. The look was meant to put him in his place, true enough, but it was a look to hide behind as well.

Those jewel eyes were bright, but they didn't sparkle. He'd seen shadows there—tiny flickerings, like something moving just beneath the surface of an icy pond. He found himself wondering what could survive those chill waters—wondering in ways that had nothing to do with computers or halfway houses.

Ryan gripped the steering wheel with both hands. Slow down, man, you'll get way off track if you don't watch it. This is about Humantec and the halfway house—period. Remember, you have to get your funding back—and you don't have a lot of time to do it.

He'd turned down one decent job offer already, and he wasn't going to turn down the next. How could he go on as a therapist when he'd failed in the worst possible way? Alicia was dead, and he hadn't been able to help her—his own little sister, and he'd done nothing.

But now, the halfway house just might have a chance. Humantec made its mistake. A small thing really. But he was going to fan it into a flame, into a roaring bonfire if that's what it took. There were lives at stake here, not just fancy technology.

TWO

Summer pulled her tool kit from her briefcase and clicked it open. Choosing the smallest in the neatly graduated row of screwdrivers, she set the kit down and swiveled the computer monitor around.

"Whew, sure is hot out there," said Roscoe, breathing heavily. He stood, red-faced, in the doorway, his forehead beaded with perspiration. "I . . . ah, just had a little chat with Dr. Jericho."

"Oh?" The screw Summer was twisting slipped and rolled under the base of the computer.

"He'll come around sooner or later," said Roscoe. "I think everything's under control now."

"Of course," she said, fishing beneath the computer for the screw and feeling it slip just beyond her fingertips.

"I see you're already installing the system."

"Hmm . . ." Her middle finger touched the top of the screw. She gave it a little flick, catching it as it rolled off the table into the palm of her other hand. "Gotcha."

"What?"

"The . . . yes. It's Humantec's policy to get the system up and running as quickly as possible." Roscoe didn't need to know she was also working off the nervous energy that had been building inside her all morning. It was like steam under pressure, and her only release was staying busy.

"Well, Ms. Keeton, is there anything I can—?"

"No . . . no. I have it all planned out. Your staff will have computers in their offices by Monday."

Roscoe tucked his thumbs into his belt. "Splendid."

"Just the hardware basics will be ready then," she said, rolling the screw tightly between her fingers. "I'll configure the operating system next week and load the office automation software the week after. Then I'll customize your data base. I can give you a copy of my schedule if you'd like."

"Oh no, not necessary. The contract is clear enough on that." He rocked back and forth on his heels.

She shook her head. Some people simply never worried about the details. She wasn't one of them. "If you'll excuse me, Mr. Williams, I—"

"It's Roscoe. Yes, do go on with it."

She watched him hurry down the hall. Something was still bothering the man. She could only hope Max was right about him. But could he handle the formidable Dr. Jericho? The question sent an odd tingle up her spine.

Quickly, she turned her attention back to the computer, knowing the work would keep her attention focused. No point in thinking of Jericho now—much too distracting.

Kneeling awkwardly in her straight skirt, she attached the network cable to the port in the back of the computer. She should've taken time to check into her hotel room and change into slacks. Usually she held her orientation sessions on a Friday and didn't begin to install the hardware until Saturday when she could work with less interruption. But today, she'd been too keyed up to consider going to a lonely room to wait out another long night.

She forced her attention back to her task. Hard work was the best cure for the uneasiness that was plaguing her tonight. Painstakingly, she checked her diagrams against the configuration of wires on the computer. But it wasn't long before her mind strayed, this time focusing on Ryan Jericho's handsome, scowling face.

A disconcerting quiver assaulted her stomach as she remembered his penetrating stare. There had been nothing soft about that look.

Just stick to your computers, she told herself with annoyance. Only computers could replace the cruel inconsistencies of human behavior with concrete, logical details.

Max once told her she had a computer in place of a heart. She'd been angry with him at the time and denied it with a slosh of wine across his face. That was two years ago. She suspected he was right. But she couldn't lie to him, she couldn't tell him she loved him.

They'd stayed partners through it, though. Humantec was too important to throw away over an emotional involvement that had gone awry. That much was clear enough from the start. It had taken a while to convince Max, but he'd finally gone on to someone else. Several someone elses actually. Funny how little it seemed to matter now.

She ran her hand over the cool, smooth surface of the monitor. Not what you'd call a friend, but most of the time, easier to be with. She and Max had developed an understanding—a necessary arrangement that kept Humantec Software going. Max was still her friend, but not her lover. It wasn't as hard as it once was. She just had to keep him at a distance. It worked—surprisingly well as a matter of fact. Staying far enough away from a situation to maintain a reasonable perspective was the key.

No doubt she would need to observe Dr. Ryan Jericho with binoculars. If anyone could confuse her, he had the most potential. He was definitely a master of the unexpected. Her first impression of him—that he was nuts—may not have been totally wrong. He seemed to have an edge about him, an edge that threatened to cut. The realization set her back to work with renewed vigor.

Hours later she grudgingly slowed her hectic pace, but only long enough for a hasty snack of cheese puffs and coffee from the vending machines.

When she finally did pull the last monitor from its cardboard cradle, her arms were trembling from fatigue.

After several moments of hunting, she found the last office on her list, tucked away from the others in its own private alcove. She'd almost missed it when she'd first studied the network diagram.

As she read the sign painted on the frosted glass, she felt the muscles in her face involuntarily contract into a grimace.

DR. RYAN JERICHO, DIRECTOR
ADOLESCENT PROGRAM.

Relax, he's not even here, she reminded herself, stepping very cautiously through the office door.

Setting the computer on the paper-strewn desk, she shook out her aching arms and surveyed the scene around her. The room didn't look like any office she'd ever seen. It was cluttered beyond belief with the kind of disorder that compelled exploration, raising more questions than answers, just as its owner had.

Shelves of thick psychology texts lined one wall, paintings another. Still, the room looked more like someone's much-lived-in den than an office. In her effort to take it all in, she stumbled clumsily over a purple bloom-covered bush, and had to steady herself against a low table. Even that was crowded with pots of snow-white vinca and red geraniums. Breathing their pleasantly sweet fragrance made her feel unaccountably comfortable.

She lingered, studying a watercolor mounted above a worn oak desk. The painting's shimmering reflections of low-hanging Spanish moss drew her mind into a cool, dark swamp scene. As she took a step backward to get a better look, she saw the tiny hole in the ceiling.

It was hardly noticeable, except to someone trying to install a computer system. The cable that should have been dangling from that hole—ready to connect the computer to the network—was missing.

Summer bit her lip. This, of all offices, had to be set up without a hitch. The guys from the phone company must have forgotten to thread it through, she thought, deciding in the same instant she wasn't going to let an oversight slow down this particular installation.

Pulling off her high heels, she hiked up her skirt and climbed onto the desk. But even stretching her five feet seven inches as far as she could, her reach stopped short of the ceiling. She glanced around the office. Surely there was something in here sturdy enough to stand on.

Several chairs, arranged in a semicircle, looked promising but they had wheels. She didn't trust her balance that much, not with muscles as tired as hers. The pile of magazines heaped into a tower in the corner of the office would have to do. She stacked them on the desk as high as she dared and tried again. Fine white dust sprinkled her face as she lifted the ceiling tile from its frame. She sneezed a half-dozen times, then shoved aside the tile and poked her head through. Stretched to her limit, she could just grab hold of the end of the neatly coiled cable.

She prayed her legs wouldn't decide to cramp as she strained at the awkward angle. Gritting her teeth, she painstakingly threaded the cable through the tiny hole.

As the end of the coil unwound, she felt her stockinged feet begin to slip on the slick magazines. Kicking out in a last-ditch effort to stay upright, she heard a low, distinctive "oof" as her heel hit something hard.

The kick caught Ryan square on the chin. He saw her tumble toward him and instinctively wrapped his arms around her waist to swing her away from the desk.

"I've got you . . . steady there." She was thinner than he'd thought. Softer too. He eased her down until she was standing in front of him, but he couldn't seem to let her go.

"You . . . you're bleeding," she whispered, touching the tiny vertical cut on his chin.

His eyes locked briefly onto hers and to his surprise he recognized his own keen interest mirrored there. But the moment was gone as quickly as it had occurred and a shield of wariness closed tightly over the delicate features tilted up to him.

He let go of her, reluctance slowing each movement. "I'm all right," he said, dabbing absently at his chin with his fingertips.

"Don't, you'll smear it. Here, let me." She pulled a neatly folded tissue from her skirt pocket and pressed it against the cut.

He noticed her hand was trembling slightly. But her face wouldn't give away another uncensured expression. "I don't believe we've been properly introduced," he said. "I'm Ryan Jericho."

She stepped back shakily as if just realizing their close proximity. "Summer Keeton." She straightened her back and offered her hand. This time it didn't tremble.

"The Humantec rep," he said, feeling her long fingers warm and firm in his grip. "Too bad we didn't get to the intros the first time we met."

"Yes, well—" She withdrew her hand and adjusted a careful smile on her full lips.

Inexplicably, it bothered him to see her recover her composure so easily. He brushed a bit of ceiling plaster from her shoulder. "What were you doing up there, anyway?" he asked.

"I wasn't bugging the place, I assure you." Her back was ramrod stiff now. "I was connecting the network. The phone company apparently didn't run this last line down." She touched the cable hanging from the ceiling.

He snorted. "I remember chasing those fellows out

of here a few days ago." Despite the firming of her jaw, he couldn't help chuckling at the memory.

"Don't guess I'll do any more chasing." He cocked his head at the jumble of computer parts and broken tile on his desk. "It looks like I'm too late anyway."

"I'll have this mess cleaned up in no time," she said, quickly gathering a handful of tile chips. "I'm really very sorry. I didn't expect anyone to be working tonight."

"Leave it. I won't be staying . . . just stopped in to pick up some paperwork. There's no need to bother with it now." Or ever, he thought. She could leave the blasted computer unhooked—he wasn't about to use it.

"Please. Let me take care of the mess." Her soothing tone was obviously intended to placate him. It irritated instead. "I didn't mean to get in your way," she said.

"You didn't?"

"I didn't intend to intrude on your work tonight." She hesitated, pursing her lips, "Humantec's goal is to have each installation run as smoothly as possible."

Her cautious selection of each word made him want to shake her. He needed to have a little heart-to-heart chat with her about Humantec, but he had to find out a few things before he tried that. He'd been studying Humantec's contract all afternoon and was beginning to see possibilities. He'd returned tonight for the system pamphlet to be sure.

"I can finish cleaning up tomorrow," Summer said brightly. "Just let me straighten this a bit and I'll be going." She adjusted the desk, toppling what remained of the stack of magazines.

A tiny noise that sounded something like exasperation emerged from her tight lips. Good, he thought as he bent to pick up a magazine. He preferred her flustered—she was almost likable then. "So you're Humantec's front line," he said, suddenly feeling perversely amiable.

"Front line, middle line, and back line," she said, not looking at him. "We're a small company . . . but ambitious."

He picked up a torn magazine and tossed it on the desk. Yeah, ambitious like cold-blooded sharks. He sat back on his heels and watched her neatly stacking the ruined magazines. No, Summer Keeton wasn't shark material. In fact, she was rather warm-blooded, if the flush to her cheeks was any indication.

"Dr. Jericho—"

"Ryan."

"Ryan. I assure you, I will make every effort to have your computer running with as little inconvenience to you as possible." She gave him a rallying smile. "And then, whenever you're ready, I'll be happy to show you everything you need to know about our system—personally. We've never had a dissatisfied customer, Dr. Jer . . . ah . . . Ryan. I'm sure you'll—"

"I'll what?" he cut in. Her professional bravado was a persistent annoyance.

"Actually . . . I could do a demo of phase one. It's not operational on the network yet, but I have a single user copy and—"

"That won't be necessary," he said, his voice crisp.

She leveled her emerald gaze at him. "You aren't going to give me a chance, are you?"

He swallowed, feeling captured by something in those eyes that pulled and pushed with equal ferocity.

In silence, he took her elbow and helped her to her feet. Lifting the stack of magazines from her arms, he placed them on his desk. He'd prepared himself to fight Humantec, but warring with this woman was making him crazy.

"Ms. Keeton, it's not a matter of giving you a chance. It's simply that I take my commitment to my clients very seriously."

She opened her mouth to speak but he went on quickly.

"Humantec is getting in the way of that commitment, and there is no way I'm going to back a system that interferes with my responsibility to my clients."

"I understand," she said, her tone honeyed. "I'm sorry this isn't what you would have chosen. But believe me, you won't be disappointed."

He didn't plan to be disappointed. There were people counting on him, and he wasn't going to back off.

The face she turned toward him was serene, only the eyes expectant. He noticed faint shadows of fatigue smudged beneath them and felt a twinge of guilt over the problems he was going to cause this plucky lady.

"I suppose I could manage to sit through one of your demonstrations . . . if it's short," he said.

When she smiled, her whole face beamed. He didn't think he'd sounded all that enthusiastic. "I'm just promising to sit through one short demo," he clarified, "and that's all."

"Terrific!" She continued smiling as she wiggled her feet back into a pair of high heels.

Her legs went on forever. He felt an urge to glide his hands along their sculptured curves. Similar musings on that same pair of legs were distracting him just about the time her heel had cropped him mercilessly on the chin.

He'd enjoyed the fantasy in the single-minded way only a man who'd been alone for a little too long would. He'd isolated himself this past year, but there'd been a time when his life had been much different. Shoving his hand through his hair, he breathed out slowly.

Summer Keeton was another matter altogether. If he was going to fight Humantec, he would have to get to know Humantec's representative better—much better.

"When will you be ready to do that demo?" he asked.

"If you'll give me an hour, I could do it tonight." Her answer was bright, full of energy he knew she didn't feel.

He shook his head. "I think I've had my dose of Humantec for one day. Another time maybe?"

Disappointment flickered across her face, quickly replaced by that smile he was beginning to hate. It covered entirely too much.

"Okay, next week then—first thing." The corners of her lips remained stubbornly upturned. "I'll be out of here in a jiffy," she said, gathering her tools and diagrams and packing them into her briefcase.

As she leaned over to close the lid, the ornate clasp that tortured her hair into its tight bun slipped loose. Watching the sudden cascade of wild curls mock her efforts at control brought him a surprising amount of enjoyment.

She struggled to twist the thick locks back into place, her fingers moving too rapidly to be effective.

When the clasp dropped a second time, she closed her eyes, and he could have sworn he heard a growl deep in her throat.

"Here, let me try." He palmed the barrette before she could protest. "Beautiful workmanship," he said, turning it over to examine the golden swirls.

"Thank you. It was . . ." Her eyes shadowed for an instant.

"Yes?" He had to watch her carefully, those brief moments before her smile took over were becoming a precious window for him.

"Family heirloom," she said vaguely and reached for the clasp.

He held it away. "I used to do this for my sister, Alicia," he said, picking up a lock of her hair. "She could never do it up by herself. Turn around. That's right." He gently positioned her shoulders, resisting the urge to massage the stiffness from them.

Letting his fingers slide through the curls, he pulled her hair up. Heavy, soft, just as he knew it would be. The dark gold curls caressed his fingers, winding around them as if they knew him well.

He felt his throat constrict and hastily twisted the shining locks into a neat ball. Securing the clasp, he brushed the remaining dust from the back of her blouse as if it were the most natural act in the world.

She murmured a tight thank-you as she patted the perfect coil.

"You're welcome," he said, focusing on her bottom lip. It was a little swollen, red. If he hadn't known better, he would have thought she'd been biting it.

"It must be getting late." Her voice was just above a whisper.

"After eleven. I think." He didn't look at his watch, too absorbed in speculating about what lay beneath the murky green of her gaze. The hint of panic he saw there told him something had her off kilter. Beautifully off kilter.

"I had no idea it was so late," she said. "I should be checking into my hotel room . . ."

"You don't have a place to stay yet?" he asked, his mind slipping back into gear.

"No. I drove straight here from Atlanta early this morning. But I have reservations."

"Where?"

"The Whitley Inn."

"Clyde Whitley's place?" He picked up her brief-case and pretended to rub at a dust spot.

"Red Oak Road—three miles off highway six on the right," she said, as if quoting a brochure.

"That's Clyde's place. But you won't get a room tonight. He closed up hours ago." Ryan flipped the briefcase handle back and forth, certain what he was going to do next was in the best interest of all concerned.

"There must be a night staff."

"Don't think so." Clyde wouldn't mind losing a little business for a good cause.

"Then I'll find a Holiday Inn or something . . ."

"Sure, but not in Sandy Flats. Closest one is in Odell—thirty miles south of here." He handed her the case and watched her shoulders sag.

"Then there's Alford Place, Carrie Alford's bed and breakfast."

Summer's eyes brightened. "She wouldn't happen to be open, would she?"

"Probably not."

"My luck."

He tried not to chuckle over how easy this was. "I might be able to persuade her to take you in, though."

"Oh?" Her tone was hopeful.

"Carrie's my aunt. I'll call and tell her we're coming," he offered graciously, pleased to see the relief on her unsuspecting face.

"Let me get my jacket. I'll be back in a sec . . ." she said, scurrying out of the office.

He laughed out loud as he reached for the phone. This should work out perfectly.

Aunt Carrie's voice twittered in his ear like a tiny bird's. "Oh la, how lovely! This is wonderful!"

He wound the phone cord around his fingers, realizing too late his inquisitive aunt Carrie would wonder about his bringing someone to Alford at this hour, especially a woman. "I am extending a professional courtesy," he said belatedly. "And that's all."

"No doubt, my dear. Whatever you say. You've been such a hermit since, well . . . I just thought—"

"It's all right." He slowly unwound the cord and sighed. "Don't wait up . . . please."

"But—"

"I can take care of everything," he said, his voice low and controlled, a tone he knew would be listened to.

"Certainly. Oh la." The receiver clicked, cutting off the soft twitter.

Ryan shook his head as he hung up, hoping he hadn't just made a mistake.

Summer appeared in the doorway, still smiling. He started to ask her if it hurt to keep those muscles in one position so long, but he thought better of it. No need to antagonize her. In fact, he needed to understand her every bit as well as Humantec if he was going to have a chance to thwart the project. The task might prove to be a little difficult, but not altogether unpleasant.

She pointed toward the gaping hole in the ceiling. "I wouldn't normally leave a mess like this—"

"It'll still be here Monday."

"Don't worry, I'll be here tomorrow. It'll be fixed before the weekend's over. And I promise not to be a bother."

He gave her a considering look. He was bothered all right, and not just by the woman's computers.

The night was black—no moon, no stars, and no lights—the deep velvety darkness of country far away from city glow.

Summer drove her van down the long, straight road through a forest of pine trees. Training her eyes on the taillights of Ryan's Jeep, she prayed she wouldn't lose track of him before they reached Alford Place.

She'd followed those tiny red lights through so many turns, she was now hopelessly lost. Her heart crept slowly to her throat. This road was entirely too lonely. She craned her neck forward, staring into the mist that hung just above the road and gritting her teeth against the eerie hollowness that wanted to settle in her stomach.

The lights ahead blinked out.

She slammed her foot on the brake and peered down her pitifully small headlight beams. Ahead, on the right, two stone pillars marked the remnants of a once-massive gate. She took a deep breath. It was her only choice. She turned off the road and through the pillars.

When the Jeep reappeared in the flood of her head-lights, a ridiculously huge wave of relief swept through her. At least he'd had the courtesy to pull off and wait. But before she'd begun to breathe again, he waved and the Jeep barreled on.

Why had it ever seemed like a good idea to follow this man into oblivion? Only because he had the disconcerting effect of blotting out her ability to reason.

She wrapped her fingers more tightly around the steering wheel. This is for Humantec, she reminded herself as the van crept slowly beneath a low archway of moss-draped oaks.

The Jeep appeared at the side of the road as she rounded a curve and guided the van to a lurching halt behind it. Closing her eyes, she waited for her heart to stop pounding.

No, she wasn't spooked at all. The feeling that threatened to dissolve her spine was strictly from exhaustion, nothing else. Anyone who'd been up since four A.M., with only a half cup of coffee and a bag of cheese puffs in her stomach, had a right to be a little skittish.

"Hey, are you okay in there?"

She jumped as the beam from Ryan's flashlight shone on her face.

"Did you have trouble? I was about to come back to get you," he said, in a tone that sounded as warm as the night.

"How much farther?" she asked, keeping her voice low to disguise its tremble.

"We're here." He opened her door and beckoned

her out with an exaggerated wave of his arm. "Alford Place, humble as it is."

Her gaze followed the narrow strip of illumination from his flashlight to a ramshackle, gray-shadowed mansion, barely visible through the trees.

"This is not exactly what I . . ."

"Had in mind? I don't imagine it was." Chuckling, he opened the van's door.

"It . . . it looks so dark," she whispered, sliding out, pulling her briefcase behind her. The house loomed, pale and haunting behind the gnarled oaks. She gripped her case to her chest to suppress a shiver. Maybe she'd made a mistake.

"What other bags do you need to take in?" he asked.

"Oh. Just a few things." A shotgun and a large guard dog for starters. Fumbling with the handle of her hanging bag, she pulled hard and barely kept from stumbling backward into his too-close chest.

Silently, he took the bag and reached out for the small suitcase she was wiggling out of its spot.

"I can get it," she said, forcing the words through the tightness in her throat.

"What about the rest of this?" he asked, looking over her shoulder at the jam-packed mass of wires and boxes in the back of the van.

"Oh, it's just some computer equipment." She gave the doors a quick shove. He didn't need to get an eyeful of that. This wasn't a good place to make him mad again.

"Are you sure this is all you need?" He gave her a wide grin instead of the derisive remark she was expecting.

The ground under her feet seemed to shift whenever his eyes focused on her like that. "Oh yes. I'm very efficient in my packing. All it takes is a little organization and planning," she said, steadying herself with a jumble of words.

"How long do you expect to be in Sandy Flats?" he asked as they followed a row of magnolia trees toward the house.

"It usually takes about six weeks, including customizing the data base." His good humor was going to be short-lived if he kept asking questions like this.

"That long?" He walked on quickly.

She couldn't read his expression well enough in the dim light to be sure, but he didn't seem to be scowling.

The darkened windows gave the house a depressingly deserted look, and Summer's stomach tightened. "It doesn't look like anyone is awake," she said as they reached the porch. "I thought you called ahead."

Ryan dangled a set of keys in front of her, and she wished more than ever she could read his face.

"No problem," he said, his voice light. "I told Aunt Carrie I'd get you settled. You'll meet her in the morning."

She nodded. A nice normal night clerk waiting to check her in would have gone a long way toward settling her nerves. But that was apparently too much to ask for. She rested wearily against a thick, vine-covered column wondering why—for that one instant when she fell from the ceiling into Ryan's arms—she'd felt so completely safe with him. She sighed. It was so much easier when all she had to worry about was the program on the computer screen in front of her.

"C'mon, Summer, it's not haunted—I promise," said Ryan as he ushered her inside.

She put down her suitcase and fought back the odd shakiness that kept creeping up on her. His reassuring smile in the glow of the small lamp that lit the foyer was comforting—until he picked up a room key from the front desk and his smile leveled into a grim line. She stood very still as he read the attached note.

"Don't tell me your aunt has no vacancies," she said, struggling to keep her voice even.

"Oh, there's a room all right." He wadded the note and quickly stuffed it into his back pocket.

"What is it?" she asked, unable to keep the apprehension out of her tone.

He slung the bag over his shoulder and picked up her suitcase. "Let's get you upstairs," he said, his baritone smoothly reassuring. "You don't look like you can stand up much longer." He motioned toward a wide staircase that curved into a balcony, his eyes softening in the shadowy light. "It's not too far. Can you make it?"

"Of course." She took her suitcase from him, not wanting to appear as wiped out as she felt. Focusing her gaze on his back, she struggled up the stairs behind him, determined to ignore the effects of the past hour's tension on her already-fatigued body. But she was barely halfway up when the broad shoulders ahead of her blurred.

She fought against the familiar light-headedness, continuing to climb step after step on sheer willpower. As she reached the balcony, she grabbed the wrought iron railing to keep from tumbling backward.

The feeling would pass, it always did. Her body

turned on her like this occasionally, rebelling against her careless attitude toward food and rest. And of course it always waited until the worst possible moment to voice its pique. She shut her eyes against the empty darkness below, willing the world to stop spinning.

"What's wrong?" Ryan asked, his voice coming from very near.

"Dizzy . . . that's all . . . happens sometimes when I skip meals." She opened her eyes and saw his face close to hers, too close. She couldn't move.

He lifted her suitcase out of her grasp and in one swift movement encircled her in his arms, pulling her against his massive chest as he eased her away from the balcony rail. "Just don't lean over," he whispered.

She could feel his warm breath on her cheek.

"As soon as you're settled, I'll get you something to eat," he said, continuing to hold her as they made their way down the hallway. She didn't protest, although she was sure she could walk on her own now. The feel of his arm wrapped securely around her waist was undeniably pleasant. For a moment, tucked into his hold, molding easily to his side, she felt she belonged there. It was a sensation far more bewildering than anything else that had happened that night.

When he stopped in front of the last room at the end of the dark hall, she felt the muscles of his powerful chest tense. It was a barely perceptible movement. Had she not been so attuned to the feel of his body next to hers, she might have missed it.

She straightened away from his grasp and studied his face through her lashes. He turned the key in the lock, and she glimpsed his unmistakable withdrawal as the door swung open. His eyes registered the change, their blue darkening, going deeper than she could hope to follow.

With a jerky motion, he flicked on a ruffle-shaded lamp beside the door. "I'll get your luggage," he said gruffly, disappearing like a ghost into the gloom of the hallway.

What just happened? Had he been planning to make a pass and changed his mind? She stared down the hall as if the shadows could answer. No, indecision didn't fit a man like Ryan Jericho.

She stepped into the room and surveyed the furnishings, wondering if they held a clue to his odd behavior. Everything looked normal enough, old but obviously treated with loving care. The burnished mahogany furniture was waxed to a shine and glowed darkly against a background of freshly painted, cream-colored walls.

She tiptoed in, unwilling to disturb the museumlike peace, and gingerly sat on the edge of the four-poster bed. As its softness beckoned her, she lay back, letting the remainder of her strength drain into the creamy delicate folds of the comforter. Running her fingers over it, she stretched, catlike, luxuriating in the homey comfort of the room. There was nothing amiss here at all.

Bathed in warm yellow lamp glow, she studied the lace canopy above her, imagining herself safe inside a cream puff. The whimsy soothed her nerves and calmed her mind.

"I'll leave these here," Ryan said, his return yanking her back from the brink of sleep. He set her luggage down, his large frame crowding the doorway. "Do you feel any better?"

"I'm fine now . . . Thanks." She watched him scan the room, as if he were looking for something. "This is a very nice bed," she said, suppressing a yawn.

The muscles in his face tightened, and she found herself automatically clutching the spread. Strange man, strange house. And she was lying here on the bed. With a quick intake of breath, she sat up. The room tilted at the sudden motion. Don't faint now, she begged, blinking against the impending spin. She wanted to stand up, but didn't trust her legs. She shouldn't give this man another opportunity to put his arms around her, however warm and solid they felt.

"You need to eat," he said, his soft, low voice easing the hardness in his face. "I'll see what's in the fridge."

He left quickly, as if he couldn't get away fast enough—definitely not the behavior of someone planning a come-on. No sense asking for trouble, though. She eased slowly up from the bed, thankful the room was no longer spinning.

With deft practice, she unloaded the contents of her suitcase into the dresser drawers and unzipped the hanging bag, arranging her suits in the armoire in minutes. The task took no thought, it seemed she'd repeated it endlessly during the four years since she'd finished college.

Pausing to listen for Ryan's footsteps, she wondered if he would deposit her snack on the doorjamb and leave as quickly as before. Torn between hoping he'd do just that and something altogether different, she smoothed the wrinkles out of her suits and adjusted them meticulously on their hangers.

She shrugged and carefully creased a dove-gray lapel before closing the armoire. She didn't need complications. Humantec was her life. It worked better that way, she told herself. Every single bit of her energy was pumped into the company she and Max had begun just after they'd graduated.

Maxwell Pelion. He'd thought they were in love. But that was a long time ago. She'd understood from the beginning that the love they shared was for their mutual project, not each other, not anything as unpredictable as that.

It was better this way. Now, Max was a friend as well as a business partner. A partner she was bound and determined not to let down. He'd worked as hard to get Humantec on its feet as she had. And the Sandy Flats contract would put them over the top.

She studied the intricate carving on the door of the armoire, resisting the urge to go back to the comfort of the cream-puff bed and pull the covers over her head.

"I see you didn't follow my advice to stay put," said Ryan disapprovingly, eyeing her unpacked suitcase. He was standing at the doorway, holding a tray of sandwiches and a tall glass of milk. "At least sit down—please," he said, hesitating before he stepped across the threshold. It was as if he'd had to force himself to enter. He put the tray on the bed, sat down, and patted the spot beside it.

She sat down carefully, trying not to topple the tray. "I . . . I'm just not comfortable until I've settled in," she said, feeling at once guilty and contrite. He didn't have to tell her what to do, even if it did make sense.

She picked up a sandwich. "Thanks. I'm sorry to keep putting you out."

"You haven't. I like looking after people."

"You do it well." Yes, she thought, he did have a way of making her feel taken care of. She fought the uncanny inclination to succumb and bit into her sandwich, studying him out of the corner of her eye. His presence filled the room, riveting all of her senses to one spot.

His gaze remained on the doorway.

"I can't possibly eat all of this," she said, uneasy with the silence between them. "Here, have one." She held out a thick-sliced ham sandwich.

"No thanks," he said, standing up abruptly as if · she'd just interrupted his thoughts. "I'll leave you alone now. You need your rest." He turned to go.

"Wait." Inexplicably, she wasn't ready for him to leave. "I . . . ah, don't exactly know where I am. Can you give me directions back to the clinic? I'll need to go in tomorrow."

"Tomorrow's Saturday," he said, his eyes following the path his hand made down the doorframe. "You ought to give yourself a day off."

"It's easier to do the networking when no one is around."

"I see." His gaze suddenly focused on her with an intensity that made her want to squirm. His grin was as unexpected as it was devastating. "Then I'll drive you."

She smiled to cover her gulp. "You don't need to do that. I can follow almost anybody's directions. I've put you to enough trouble already and—"

"No trouble. I don't live far from here. I'll swing by and get you on my way into town. Nine o'clock?"

"That's awfully late—"

"You can use the extra sleep."

"But—"

"Now, finish your sandwich, get in that bed, and give yourself some dream time." His soft command hung in the air long after he had gone, disturbing any notion of sleep Summer might have had.

THREE

Damn these early mornings. "When did they leave?" asked Ryan.

"A good half hour ago, maybe more," said the dark, silver-haired man, stacking another breakfast dish.

"Where'd they go?" He wished he'd had a chance to talk to Aunt Carrie before she'd commandeered Summer.

"Ah, so it's the young lady that pulled you outta tha' swamp so early. My, my . . ." The old man eyed him with a grin but did not pause from his task.

"Marcus, I'm here to take Ms. Keeton to the clinic," said Ryan. "It's just business." He helped himself to a biscuit, spreading it thick with butter and momentarily letting his appetite override his worry.

"Uh-huh. On a Saturday? Now that's curious. You been holing up all by your lonesome and now it's business and it just happens to have a real pair of legs. Reckon Carrie's as curious as I am, seeing as how you bring the lady here in the middle of the night."

"What did Aunt Carrie say to you?" asked Ryan, closing his eyes as he bit into the biscuit.

"It's not me she's talkin' to this morning. I 'magine she's got a few questions for our new guest." Marcus chuckled. "Yep. She was just chattering away last time I saw her."

Ryan coughed loudly, choking on a mouthful of biscuit. "Where'd they go?"

"The garden, I 'magine. You know your aunt well as I do."

Downing a glass of orange juice, Ryan nodded. He should've expected as much. Aunt Carrie's attention was evenly divided between her passion for flowers and her unabashed interest in other people's business. It was the latter that concerned him now. "I'd better find them," he said, heading toward the French doors that led from the dining room to the back terrace.

"What's your hurry, son?" asked Marcus, wiping his hands on a towel as he double-stepped to match Ryan's stride.

"Ah . . . no hurry . . . just want to get on to the clinic."

Marcus raised his eyebrows. Ryan surreptitiously scanned the gardens, trying hard not to feed the old man's curiosity further. From the veranda he could see the head-high line of gardenia hedges that spread in a labyrinth from the house to the river below. There was no one on the brick paths.

"Since when did you ever bother to be on time?" Marcus squinted at him skeptically. "You tryin' to make some kind of impression on your lady friend?"

"Yes. But it's strictly professional."

"I saw Ms. Keeton myself, ya' know." Marcus

laughed softly. "Professional . . . uh-huh." His grin stretched wide.

Marcus Murphy had been at Alford Place ever since Ryan could remember and was as good at digging as Aunt Carrie—and not only in the garden. "Ms. Keeton's an interesting woman," said Ryan noncommittally. He knew he'd acted more on impulse than reason in bringing Summer here. He would just have to make sure Aunt Carrie and Marcus understood the situation.

"So you got an interestin' lady friend, eh? 'Bout time you—"

"Maybe they went down to the river," he said quickly, stepping down from the veranda before Marcus could probe further. "Can't let Aunt Carrie keep Ms. Keeton traipsing around in those flowers all morning."

He breathed deeply of the warm, bloom-scented air as he walked down the path. So he did make the decision to bring her here from his gut, not his brain. He should take that as proof he'd done the right thing.

He smiled at the memory of Summer falling out of the ceiling into his arms. She'd been lighter than he'd expected—fragile. She acted tough, but just how tough was she? One thing he was certain of, she didn't know how to take care of herself. Much too thin, and probably overworked. She was a walking zombie by the time they got here last night. It was a good thing he'd been around to help her to her room.

He pushed his fingers through his hair with an exasperated motion. You're crazy, Jericho. You don't need to be thinking about taking care of her. Forget it. You're not so good at that anymore . . . remember?

He pulled a leaf from the gardenia hedge, and tore

it slowly as he walked. He'd learned quite a bit going over the Humantec pamphlet last night, even if it was covered in water spots. Summer had a lot of work ahead of her. Maybe just a little too much. All he had to do was slow down her progress. It was a plan, of sorts.

Roscoe did say the contract change was last minute. And Summer didn't seem to be aware of it. Admittedly, the scheme had a slim chance of succeeding. But hell, what choice did he have? Persuade Summer Keeton to see his point of view? Worth a try, but highly unlikely.

"My goodness, Ry boy, you're out early," said Aunt Carrie as she slipped gracefully through an opening in the hedge.

Enough was enough. "Can't a person get up early every once in a while without everybody commenting on it?" said Ryan more sharply than he'd intended.

She adjusted her wide-brimmed strawhat. "No need to bark like a big dog. The change obviously doesn't agree with you."

"Sorry, Aunt Carrie." He hugged her warmly. "I was . . ."

"Mulling over something. I can tell, just look what you've done to that leaf."

He tossed the green shreds into the hedge. "Where's Ms. Keeton? Marcus told me you two were together."

"Picking zinnias," she said brightly, shoving a basket overflowing with blossoms into Ryan's arms.

"She is? I didn't think she was the flower-picking type," said Ryan.

"So tell me, what do you know about our Summer girl?" she asked, obviously hoping for a complete biography.

"A lot less than you do by now." He tucked two red zinnias into the band of his aunt's hat and smiled as she fingered the arrangement. "I hope you haven't been cross-examining her."

"Now, Ry, I'm just making friends," she said sweetly. "You've chosen well, dear. She's a lovely—"

"Hold it right there." He put his hands up, as if the motion alone would cease her ridiculous notions. "The woman is only working at the clinic for a few weeks. I'm being hospitable."

She smiled at him, her blue eyes twinkling. "Of course, my dear."

"Don't make it what it's not," he said firmly. As well-meaning as Aunt Carrie was, it was sometimes difficult getting through to her. But this time he had to make her understand. "I mean it. Do not interfere . . . you've done enough already."

"What have I done? A walk in the garden, a little chitchat?"

"You put her in Alicia's room—on purpose. Don't deny it."

She took the basket from him. "I'm not making the room into a shrine," she said quietly.

"But after all that happened in there—"

"Summer seems like a practical woman. I don't think it will bother her." Aunt Carrie's long, filmy dress shimmered in the sunlight as she spoke, the tremoring movement the only testament to her emotions. "It isn't the room that holds on to the demons, Ry, my darling, it's you."

Ryan pressed his lips together in a tight line, unable to deny the truth in her words.

She stroked his cheek, just as she had when he'd needed comfort as a small boy.

He took her gnarled hand, pulling it gently away. "I'd rather you not discuss certain things with our guest," he said gruffly, feeling his chest tighten.

"As you wish, Ry." She mimicked his steely-eyed look for a quick moment. Then her lips curled back into a grin as Summer pushed awkwardly through the hedge. "Ah, lovely Summer girl," she singsonged.

Ryan squeezed his aunt's hand warmly before he dropped it, trusting the touch to convey his hope for her understanding.

The night's rest had erased all traces of Summer's fatigue. Arms laden with zinnias of all colors, she looked disturbingly radiant.

He shook his head, trying to bring back the tailored business professional he'd met yesterday. Yes, the Humantec rep was there, hair confined, clothes pressed stiff. But for an instant, he thought he saw something else. Her smile. Was it actually shining in her eyes now? The notion was intriguing.

"Good morning," said Summer, glad to find she wasn't lost. Thank goodness she'd seen Ryan's dark head above the hedge. Carrie Alford had managed to make her feel totally welcomed, but she was as difficult to keep up with as Ryan himself.

She looked at the two pairs of blue eyes trained on her, similar, but one a deeper shade, more intent than the other. "Your aunt has the most wonderful garden— it's absolutely gorgeous," she said breathlessly. "I could just stay here all day, forever for that mat—" Her mouth clamped shut over the babble of words. It was only the fresh air making her so giddy.

"I see Aunt Carrie already has you under her spell," said Ryan, regarding her with an amused look. "She's brought people out here who've never been seen again."

"Oh pooh. Don't you believe that." Carrie fluttered her eyelids in mock haughtiness. "Anyone with any sensitivity at all can't resist the magic of my flowers."

Ryan laughed. "Resist it, Summer . . . with all your might, or you'll be lost forever."

Summer wasn't prepared for the warmth that rolled through her when she saw the mirth in his face. Such a change from the barely controlled tempest that had tightened his features the day before. "Is this where the plants in your office came from?" she asked, trying to slow the disconcerting thump of her heart.

"Yes. Aunt Carrie lets me keep a bit of her magical garden at the clinic," he said, his eyes still registering humor but focusing intently on her.

She turned quickly to Carrie. "I . . . I've never seen such utterly beautiful plants, their colors are so vivid."

"That's because there's powerful enchantment here. Don't ever doubt it," Carrie said, plucking a blossom from the hedge. She twirled it in front of her impish face, inhaling deeply. "Spirits dance in my garden. You can feel them, soft and warm, like the flower's scent."

Summer held her breath as she watched Carrie play with the white bloom. In spite of herself, she half-believed the woman's prattling. There was an undeniably strange feeling in the air. She couldn't help imagining a capricious spirit, a naked cherub, hiding in the gardenia hedge. The giggle that slipped out was unstoppable.

"Why, Aunt Carrie, I do believe one of your garden ghosts just tickled Summer," said Ryan.

Summer made the mistake of looking at him again. His blue-black hair, shining in the sun, framed by gardenia blossoms, made him seem like an otherworldly creature himself. She watched him drape his arm tenderly across Carrie's shoulders. His chambray shirt partially unbuttoned and rolled up at the sleeves revealed tanned, muscular forearms.

She turned to Carrie, her breathing strangely ragged. "So . . . so you think there are really magical beings in your garden?"

"I don't just think it, Summer one, I feel it in my soul. You must feel it too." The old woman smiled mischievously. "Here, Ry," she said, holding up the gardenia blossom, "twine this into Summer's braid, like you did my hat."

"I don't think . . . You don't have to . . ." Summer felt the warmth of his body as he stepped close. Staring at the zinnias in her sweaty hands, she held her breath and stood deathly still as he tugged gently on her hair to place the flower.

"Perfect," he said, surveying his handiwork, then winked at her as if they shared a secret.

The heat rising in Summer's cheeks warned her she was about to blush, a flaw she'd always hated. She tried desperately to suppress it now.

"Here, let me take those flowers for you, dear," said Carrie, easing the crushed stems from her grasp. "I'll go find a vase to put them in." She floated back up the path. "I'm sure you two have better things to do than wander in a poor old woman's garden all day," she said as her dress melted into the foliage.

"Have you seen the river yet?" asked Ryan, as if nothing were amiss.

"No. Maybe I'll get a chance another time." She had to concentrate to slow her heartbeat. "We'd better go or it'll be noon by the time we get to the clinic," she said, thankful her words miraculously sounded crisp and businesslike.

Ryan cocked his head to one side and smiled at her. "You did say you'd be in Sandy Flats for six weeks, right?"

She looked at a leaf just beyond his left ear. "Yes. But—"

"Do you really want to spend a glorious day like this inside—with a computer?"

No. But she couldn't spend another moment standing in the fragrant heat of a magical garden with this man or she'd make a fool of herself.

"I have a lot to get done," she said briskly. "I can't—"

"You can." The words were soft but compelling. "Let me show you the river," he urged. "There's a canoe in the boat house. We could go out for just a little while—before it gets too hot."

"I ought to get to work—"

"One single day won't make much difference. Will it?"

She worried the gardenia blossom in her hair with one hand and smoothed her pale green slacks with the other. She should have been at the clinic hours ago. "I suppose I could take a few minutes to see the river, and make up for it with a long day tomorrow."

No . . . no, the network should be set up today, she thought, feeling herself float irresistibly into a pair of shimmering blue eyes. "I suppose I could still stay on schedule if I start early enough Sunday."

"Forget the schedule," Ryan said, his grin summoning her, "at least for a little while."

Summer trailed her fingers in the cool water, knowing she shouldn't be enjoying herself nearly as much as she was. But there was something here that thoroughly sapped her drive to work. It flowed into her veins, pouring its peacefulness over her plans and schedules, obliterating all urgency.

The river ruled now, setting their pace, determining their direction. Its currents moving lazily around the swollen trunks of the cypress trees that stood immovable in its path.

"Shall we go upriver, or down?" Ryan asked. He sat in the canoe's stern, sculling with the only paddle they'd been able to find.

"Upriver," she said, fighting the sweet lethargy that pulled at her coherence.

"Good choice. We'll head toward Prescot's Landing," he said, bringing the canoe around with a swift stroke. "The current will be with us on the way back."

She nodded, watching the tiny water bugs skim across the canoe's path.

"Hey, is that a snake over there?" said Ryan, motioning with his paddle to a point just beyond her fingers.

Summer jerked her hand out of the water and clamped it over her mouth before the cry of alarm could escape. Swallowing hard, she turned around in time to catch his devilish grin.

"No, guess not," he said, smirking. "Must have been a stick. Better stay alert, though." He was all innocence now. "You're not afraid of snakes, are you, Summer?" His eyes twinkled like his aunt's.

"No. Of course not." She gulped, silently vowing to return the scare he'd given her. "But I don't like to take chances."

"I'll bet you don't."

"What do you mean by that?" She shifted in her seat to face him. He was still smiling.

"You're always prepared, aren't you?" he said. "I'll bet you were a good Girl Scout."

"As a matter of fact, I was." She sat up straighter. "But it was my father who taught me to be prepared. He knew how to make sure you didn't forget to take care of all the details."

Ryan leaned forward, his expression thoughtful. "Pretty strict with you, eh?" His low, gentle voice tugged at her, encouraging her to go on.

"Yes, I suppose. He was a marine—used to giving orders and having them followed. Mother died when I was twelve." Here she was, rattling on again. Why in the world had she told him that?

"Must have been rough," he said.

"We managed." She sucked in her breath and stared at the sun-dappled wall of foliage ahead. She never talked about her personal life, with anyone, ever. What was it about Ryan that made her brain quit but the words keep coming?

"Are you all right?" He lifted the paddle out of the water, resting it across his lap.

"Sure," she said, constructing what she hoped was a convincingly lighthearted smile. "Of course." She thought of her mother who had offered so much warmth and affection, the only tangible evidence of love she'd ever known. But she was gone forever, and it was her father's lessons she'd finally mastered, learning to bear her grief in dignified silence.

Summer forced her cheerful face to remain intact, careful to keep a lift to her chin despite the dip in her spirits. She watched the angles of Ryan's rugged face soften in the filtered light and noticed his eyes had deepened a shade. Desperate for a diversion, she turned her smile on full force. "Now that I've got your attention, I'd like to tell you about Humantec's system."

His brows arched in surprise.

"That isn't what we were talking about."

"Humantec is what I want to talk about," she countered.

"You came all the way out here, into the swamp, in this little canoe, to tell me about Humantec?" He looked at the paddle in his hands as if it could explain. "Is this woman serious?"

"I seize an opportunity where I see it," she said, biting her lip as the sun glinted off the tips of his dark lashes.

"Humantec is my . . . that is, I programmed the system—most of it anyway. Custom-tailored data bases are our specialty," she said, trying in vain to remember her usual speech, the one to win over hardened skeptics. "I can answer any questions you have," she finished, her mind emptying under his stare. "So . . . do you have any, ah . . . questions?"

He dipped the paddle and slowly pulled it through the water, his shirt tightening over the muscles in his shoulders. "I want to know about Summer Keeton."

"The custom designing was my idea," she said, determined to keep the conversation on work. "I planned it as a shell, sort of." Her stockpile of information melted into a warm pool at the bottom of her stomach as she tried to think. "I can . . . ah . . . program special things, functions, to suit any buyer." So it wasn't her tried-and-true speech—it was all her brain could produce.

"You must spend a lot of time sitting in front of a computer," said Ryan, his smile charmingly lopsided.

"Not as much as I used to," she said, swallowing hard. "Now, I spend so much time traveling, I don't get to work on the programs like I should."

She'd done it again, talking to this man about things she'd hardly admitted to herself. It was completely irrelevant anyway. She had to do what was best for Humantec, and that meant traveling anywhere she had to, to install a system.

"Humantec's success is very important to me," she said, emphasizing each word for her own benefit as well as his. "I'm happy to do anything to promote it." She smoothed her cotton slacks and straightened her back.

"I don't think I'd be able to buddy up with a computer for very long," said Ryan, watching her with an expression that could have been teasing or pitying. It was exasperating not to be sure. "I wouldn't want to be away from home all the time. Mighty lonely. I prefer to stay in one spot . . . like this swamp here. She's not always predictable, but I've been with her long enough to understand her quirks."

"What do you mean?" asked Summer, seeing her chance to lead the conversation away from her.

"The river changes through here from time to

time," the sweet, low voice told her, "but it's not hard to find your way—as long as you stay where you can detect a current."

A bird screeched, beating its wings overhead, and Summer glimpsed a streak of red against the mottled canopy above as a loud ratta-tat-tat echoed through the forest.

"A pileated woodpecker," said Ryan. "There's its mate." He pointed to a large black-and-white form on a tree above them.

Summer watched Ryan's dark hair ruffle haphazardly across his forehead. Something inside her quivered as if the warm breeze was reaching beneath skin and bone. A need began to grow deep within her, a curious need to know this man, to understand him in ways that had nothing to do with the business of computers. "Have you lived in Sandy Flats all your life?" she asked, forcing her interest below the surface of a pleasantly benign smile.

"No. When I was young, I lived at boarding school. But my spirit has always been here."

"Boarding school? You?"

"Several in fact. Don't look so incredulous. What did you think? That I rose up out of the mud and ran wild in the swamp?"

Summer snickered. "As strange as it seems, that had crossed my mind."

"No doubt it would have been better than some of those schools," he said, looking at her warmly. "I did escape to the swamp in my mind even when I couldn't roam it in person."

"Why did you go to boarding school?"

"Not much choice. My father was a banker. He

traveled all over the world. Mother couldn't bear the thought of being away from him, so she followed wherever he went. It wouldn't have been much of a life for us kids." He leaned hard into his next paddle stroke. "My sister, Alicia, and I explored all along these channels when we visited Aunt Carrie every summer."

Lulled by his languid baritone, Summer relaxed against the canoe's bow and listened to the soothing voice that blended so easily with the forest sounds around them.

As the canoe rounded a bend, a turtle sunning on a wide log, plopped into the water. Summer closed her eyes and tilted her chin toward the sun, feeling its warmth soak down to her core. "It would be nice to stay here forever," she said dreamily, "just basking on a log, like that turtle, thinking about nothing at all."

Ryan gave a low chuckle that poured over her like molasses. "Now that surprises me."

"Why?" She peered at him through eyes opened a bare slit against the brightness.

He had unbuttoned his shirt, exposing a wide chest sprinkled with dark hairs that glistened in the sun. He trailed his paddle, guiding the canoe around a sandbar. Summer's muscles, a second earlier soft as melting butter, tensed unexpectedly at the sight. She closed her eyes and took a steadying breath before she spoke again. "Wh . . . Why shouldn't I want to stay here?"

"You're the type who rushes through life," he said. "Always on the move toward bigger and better."

"What's so wrong with staying on top of things?" She sighed deeply to relieve the tightness gripping her stomach. "It's the only way to succeed in this world, Ryan."

"Oh?" His mocking grin was disconcerting. "That doesn't sound like very much fun to me. I believe I'd much rather see you sunning on a log than working on a computer." He dipped his paddle and gave the canoe a strong push against the current.

"I suppose you'd like to see me do anything besides install Humantec's system." She studied the crease that was forming between his dark brows.

"The clinic isn't ready to invest in a system like Humantec's," he said with a certainty that made her uneasy.

"But we're here," she said stiffly. "Someone must think you're ready." The sudden chill in his gaze made her pause.

"And someone played a clever game of politics," he said, running his thumb over the paddle's handle.

She propped her leg on the gunwale, forcing her taut body into a relaxed position. "And you have a problem with our tactics."

"I do."

The air between them felt thick and much too warm. She licked her drying lips. "Fair enough, Ryan. But here we are. Honestly, I don't see why you're acting like Humantec is going to bring your clinic to ruin. It's just a computer system, designed to help you do your job better."

He rolled his eyes in obvious disbelief.

"Humantec is more than office automation," she continued doggedly. "It's data bases full of information, places to refer your clients, services available, whatever you need at the touch of a button." She swiped at a wisp of hair that tickled her cheek, and his gaze followed her movements. She stilled her hand immediately.

"We . . . We've even integrated with psych test software," she said, determined to quell the giddy feeling those intense cobalt eyes caused. "You give one of your clients a test, feed the raw scores to the computer, print a descriptive report and voilà, you have both diagnosis and treatment procedures in your hand."

"And voilà, you've got a diagnosis with as much insight as a machine." He slapped the paddle gently on the water, sending a cool spray arcing over them.

She wiped the mist from her eyes. He wasn't even trying to understand. "I concede a computer can't take the place of human intervention," she said, grappling with her temper as if it were a beast to be caged. Where was her usual calm?

Try one more time. "Ryan, having these capabilities can mean more freedom for you." She searched in vain for even the smallest spark of interest to light his eyes. "You'll be able to spend more time with your clients and less time writing reports . . ."

Her words trailed off. It was clear she was not making her point. Confused, she swiftly reviewed each word of their conversation. Where had she lost him? Had she been so wrapped up in her own struggle to remain composed that she'd missed something? She stared at a dragonfly inspecting her knee, unwilling to look up until she was sure he would not see her frustration. How could this man so easily, and so consistently, disrupt her thinking?

"I can see I'm not very convincing today," she said, afraid to let her silence lengthen into fear. "Suppose you tell me why Humantec is such a horrible monster."

And then he smiled.

It was the widest, most enchanting smile she'd ever seen, exposing gleaming white teeth and taking her completely by surprise.

"Well?" she said, to take up the slack in her jaw.

He chuckled.

"I know you have a problem with Humantec," she said, resisting the urge to squirm in her seat. "You just need to—"

He was laughing out loud now. "You're awfully pushy for someone who could—what was it?—bask on a log forever . . ."

"Ryan Jericho, you're just baiting me."

"You, my dear, brought the can of worms." His cockeyed smile tugged relentlessly at her senses.

"I could argue that," she said, not feeling in the least like arguing.

His gaze steadied on her in a silent plea. "Let's forget about computers for today."

She tried once more. "I want to know why you think Humantec—"

"We agreed not to talk about computers."

"We did not—"

"Are you always this persistent?"

Summer pressed her lips together. She would have to reevaluate her approach. He was much too adept at twisting the conversation away from her. "All right, I won't mention Humantec again," she agreed, "if you'll just—"

"Hey, what's that over there?" he said, pointing his paddle toward the water just below her dangling foot.

"I already fell for that one," she said, leaving her foot perched on the edge of the canoe. But to be on the safe side, she craned her neck to look where he had pointed. "I don't see a thing—"

Too late, she heard the paddle slap the water hard, drenching her blouse through to her skin.

"Give me that paddle," she demanded, returning his malicious grin.

"Do I look like an idiot?" he asked, calmly holding it out of her reach.

She dipped her hand over the side of the canoe and tried to splash him back, a maneuver that wasn't at all effective.

He slapped the paddle down again.

"You don't play fair!" she shouted, wiping the water from her face. She leaned over the gunwale as far as possible to scoop with both hands—not realizing her mistake until the murky water rushed toward her face as the canoe tipped.

FOUR

As Summer kicked to the surface, she felt Ryan's arms go around her, pulling her up in a strong, swift movement. "I can swim," she gasped when she'd finally stopped coughing. Her feet touched the mushy bottom, and she stood, the water barely coming to her shoulders. He still held her tightly.

"Th . . . The canoe," she whispered, unable to move. His eyes held hers a moment longer and then he let her go, easily catching up with the canoe as it drifted aimlessly in the slow current. She was not cold, but she shivered just the same, hugging herself against the rush of feelings that had surprised her at his touch.

"I'm sorry," she said when he returned, hoping she'd regained her composure enough not to appear rattled.

He picked his shirt out of the water as it floated by and wrung it out, giving her a mock stern look as he tossed it up on a nearby sandbar. "Nice going, lady," he said, pulling a twig from his hair, his lips curling.

A strange giddiness bubbled up in her, impossible to

ignore. "I had to make an effort to get you back," she said, trying to keep a straight face between nervous giggles.

His grin broadened until he was chuckling along with her. "You certainly know how to throw yourself into your . . . ah . . . efforts," he said, "but I think you've just upped the stakes in this game."

She tried to answer but hiccuped instead.

Laughing, he shook his head and waded to the canoe's stern. "Now how about helping me get the water out of this thing," he said, motioning her toward the bow. "Grab hold and we'll flip on the count of three. Got it?"

She hiccuped again. "Got . . . it."

"One, two, three, over!" The canoe rolled hull up.

She pulled a sopping strand of hair out of her eyes and stared. "Now what?"

"I thought you told me you were a good Girl Scout," he said through his lopsided grin. "Didn't they teach you how to empty a swamped canoe?"

She shrugged, unable to remember ever swamping a canoe before, she'd always been so careful.

"Swim underneath the bow and wait for me in the air pocket there," he said. "I'll tell you when to lift."

Obediently, she ducked and came up in the narrow space between the waterline and the upturned hull. As her eyes adjusted to the muted green light, she listened to the soft echoes of water lapping against the canoe, feeling strangely isolated from the sun and warmth above.

"Ryan?" she said, her voice sounding too loud inside the aluminum hull. His wet face broke the surface of the water, inches away from her own. Water droplets beaded on his dark lashes and brows. She watched as one trickled slowly down his rugged cheek, its path just missing his mouth.

"I thought I was supposed to get the bow," she whispered.

"So you were." He didn't move. "Now, how can we even the score here?" he asked, his tone full of suggestion.

Her throat constricted. "Wh . . . What do you mean?" she said, her voice coming out like a croak as she felt the warmth of his breath caress her cheek.

He chuckled. "I hardly think a little cooling splash with a paddle warrants a dunking in the swamp."

"That was an . . . an accident," she said shakily. "I didn't mean to—"

"Of course you didn't. But you did, and it's my turn now." His leg skimmed against hers.

She froze, her senses mesmerized. "We'll go back and . . . I'll paddle the whole way. That will even the score."

He chuckled again, low and smooth. When he touched her, she flinched, but as he traced a slow, scalding path down her jaw with his index finger, she felt something deep inside her slip. Her heart dangled loose, quivering in the core of her body, waiting to be set right.

"Summer."

She closed her eyes. "Yes?"

"What if I'm not ready to go back yet?"

She forced herself to look at him again, only to be hypnotized by his lips—so close, moist, warm, determined. She saw them part and felt his hand at the back of her neck, drawing her to him with an insistent, irresistible pressure.

His lips grazed hers, warm and gentle, a tender touch coaxing her into a trembling response that strengthened with each passing second. She had the uncanny feeling she was willing this to happen, as if a part of her was directing his every move. But when his kiss deepened, tugging at that waiting spot deep within her, she found her senses going far beyond anything her imagination had prepared her for.

An unbidden heat rippled through her body as his tongue nudged and probed. Beyond thought, she opened to him, melting into the sensuous feel of his warm, wet body against hers as his embrace tightened. She no longer had the presence of mind to orchestrate her own actions, nor could she pretend to control the man who was making every nerve thirst for sensation.

His fingers trailed from her shoulders down to the small of her back. Barely formed thoughts faded, as his hands and lips infused her with their powerful narcotic. Her consciousness adrift, her body allowed the sensual drug full reign.

Ryan lifted his head, his hot blue gaze searching, suspending time.

A loud thud on the canoe's hull yanked Summer back from her dream world. A distinctive slither was followed by a small splash. She slipped out from under the canoe just as a black serpentine form glided swiftly past her toward the opposite bank.

"Water moccasin," said Ryan, wading up behind her.

"Oh." She shivered.

He looped his arm around her waist.

She pulled away, stumbling. "No . . . I . . ."

He caught her, only holding on long enough to keep her from slipping in the mud.

"Please," she said. "I was . . . I mean . . . we shouldn't be . . ." She felt herself blushing hotly.

He made no further move toward her. "Well, I guess that makes us even now," he said, his insatiable grin creeping back.

"What?"

"The kiss. Now we don't have to go back, and you don't have to paddle."

"But I'm all wet."

"You'll dry." He plucked the battered gardenia from what remained of her braid and started to untangle the hopeless mass.

"Don't," she said, wishing she didn't sound so frantic. But she knew she couldn't let him touch her again. The feel of his hands in her hair would only blank her mind again, and the possibilities were frightening. She had almost let herself get completely out of control. If it hadn't been for the snake. . . .

"Just . . . stay over there," she said, putting her hands in front of her to ward him off. She needed time to think about what had happened, time to figure it out, analyze it. Maybe she was just overreacting. Maybe she was coming down with a fever or something. Whatever it was, the one thing she knew for certain was she had to keep away from Ryan until she could regain control of her wayward body.

Amusement played across his face, his eyes softening.

Summer grit her teeth against his irresistible lure. She had been kissed often enough, even made love to, but never without being fully aware of everything she was doing. Even in the early days when she thought she was in love with Max, she had never allowed her thoughts to become quite so detached.

"We'd better turn the canoe back over," he suggested casually, his lips continuing to hold a faint curl.

She waded to her end of the canoe, fighting her embarrassment as she ducked back under. To her relief, this time he surfaced well toward the other end.

"When I give the signal, push up and over as hard as you can," he said. "We'll flip it toward the sandbar. Ready?"

She nodded, now feeling claustrophobic in the tiny air pocket. She waited for him to give the signal, trying to meet his eye and cursing herself for not being able to.

"Well?" she asked after waiting several excruciatingly long seconds.

"I don't know whether to apologize or try to kiss you again," he said.

"Don't."

"Which?"

"Either." She wanted to get away from him and at the same time be crushed in his arms.

"I can live with that . . . for a while," he said, the glint in his eyes promising the truce would not last long.

"Are we ready to flip this thing?" she asked, desperately needing to slow the wild coursing of her blood. She shouldn't be responding to Ryan Jericho like this. Too much was at stake here to let unreliable, irrational emotions take over.

"Ready to flip. One, two, three . . . now!"

With a swift heave, the canoe flipped and came down to float beside them, empty of water.

When they were both settled back in, he sculled the paddle, keeping the craft from drifting with the current. "Do you want to go on or turn back?" he asked.

"Go on," she said, rising to the challenge in his voice. She would not let him know how unnerved she really was.

The canoe skimmed over the black water, and she could feel her pulse begin to steady as she took long, slow breaths.

He broke the silence first. "Are you afraid of snakes?"

She looked back over her shoulder at him, his eyebrows raised in innocence.

"No," she said from behind the curtain of hair she was combing with her fingers.

"What is it you're so frightened of, Summer Keeton?"

Her finger caught on a tangle. "Do you mean, is it you?" She yanked at it in frustration. "Ow!"

"Is that an answer?"

"Yes . . . no." The only thing she knew for sure was that the experience had both alarmed and tantalized her to the bone.

"What is it then?"

She tilted her chin up, a stall against his probing. "It's just that I was . . ." Jeez, c'mon, Summer, start thinking now. "Why are you so dead set against Humantec's system?" she said, and then held her breath.

Ryan frowned. "So it's back to Humantec again, is it?"

She nodded, still not breathing.

"Humantec Software Incorporated . . ." His words came slowly. The shift in his tone, the way he ground the name between his teeth, made her instantly regret her choice of topic.

"Humantec has no business in Sandy Flats," he stated evenly.

"But we're here, you can't change that," she said.

"I think I can. And I'm going to try. Summer, if you could just try to see the whole picture. If you understood, you would—"

"No, I wouldn't. This isn't the first time Humantec has met with opposition. But we've proven to be the best choice for every site we've entered. I can show you—"

"I'm not interested in other clinics," he said with hard-edged calm. "I'm interested in Sandy Flats, and we need other things a lot more than computer systems."

"I'm sure that's true," she said softly. "But Humantec isn't what's standing in your way."

"The hell it isn't."

"My experience has been that worthwhile projects get funded, sooner or later. This is Humantec's time. And I'm sure that later—"

"Summer, there isn't going to be a later—"

"Now hold on, Ryan. If you brought me here to talk me out of doing my job, you've wasted your time," she said quickly. "If you think you can kiss me and expect that to make some kind of difference, you're wrong, Ryan Jericho." She clenched her teeth over the sob that wanted to escape. She had her pride.

"Didn't you agree to come out here just to convince

me Humantec wasn't the bad guy?" he asked gently, lifting the paddle out of the water and resting it across his knees.

That had been the idea, essentially. But she hadn't planned on being kissed, or enjoying it, or wanting to do it again. No, that wasn't part of the plan at all. She bit her lip. But Ryan didn't need to know it. "So I'm guilty of wanting your support for the system," she said, with as much nonchalance as she could muster. "It looks to me like we both came out here to do some convincing."

"Maybe so." He tilted his head back, studying her. "But I also wanted to find out what kind of woman I'm dealing with." His statement was a disconcerting challenge.

She was beginning to wonder that very thing herself. What had always seemed so clear was suddenly muddled in her mind. She sat very still, the warmth draining from her body, leaving her icy cold. She had to fight this strange confusion. "Look, Ryan, I am Humantec's representative and—"

A shadow flickered across his face. "I believe there is a lot more than that beneath the coat of armor you're wearing," said Ryan.

"What?"

"It's tough, but not impenetrable."

Her heart caught at a lump in her throat. She forced her words around it. "Humantec's computer system is—"

"We have plenty of time to discuss your system." He leaned toward her. "For right now though, I'd like to separate Summer Keeton from Humantec . . ."

She forced herself to look away from the dark sprinkling of hair across his chest and concentrated on squeezing the water from her shirttails. "And can you separate Ryan Jericho from Sandy Flats clinic?" she asked.

He paused for a few moments before he answered. "When I care about people, my clients or anybody else, I get involved," he said with an odd tone of capitulation. "I'll admit the separation isn't always clear. But my work is about people—not machines—living, breathing, feeling human beings who can laugh and grow, or hurt and fail."

An uneasiness settled heavily over Summer. She sensed he'd made a confession he wasn't entirely happy with. She watched Ryan closely, wondering what had caused the sudden rigidness in his jaw. But he was focused inward now, his expression inscrutable and she knew his sun-burnished face would reveal nothing more.

Unwilling to press him, she leaned back and closed her eyes, listening to the steady, soothing swish of his paddle as the dampness steamed from her clothes.

Ryan sat on the low dock with his feet planted firmly in the canoe, keeping it from drifting away as he watched Summer's sleeping face. He hadn't expected his task of diverting her attention from her project to be quite so enjoyable. And now he was almost certain he'd been handed an extra bonus. Summer didn't seem to know that she had only four weeks to install the system instead of the usual six.

Looking down at her beautiful, unsuspecting face, he felt a sharp pang of guilt. He had no choice, he told himself. But that didn't make him feel any better about it.

He'd thought he understood the rules to the game they were playing. But now, he wasn't so sure. He pulled on his shirt and buttoned it slowly. He couldn't afford to think too hard about what he was doing. It was already too late for that.

"Wake up, sleepyhead," he said, shaking her shoulder gently.

"Wh . . . What?"

He watched her eyes flutter open and stare at him groggily. Lord, he'd never get used to that shade of green. What would it be like to wake up in the morning to that? "We're at Prescot's Landing," he said.

She sat up, stretching like a graceful cat, her tousled hair framing a sleepily sexy expression. What a change from the brilliant but stilted computer programmer.

He could get used to this side of Summer Keeton. He smiled to himself, despite his misgivings. "We can get some lunch here before we start back," he said as he offered his hand.

Summer glanced down at her dry but very wrinkled blouse. "Wait. I can't go in looking like this."

He cleared his throat. "You look perfect."

She hesitated.

"Old Jimmy's most likely the only person in there," he said. "You'll sure give him something to gossip about to his fishing buddies." This time he didn't wait for a response. Taking her hand, he pulled her up out of the canoe.

"Well, if it ain't Dr. Jericho hisself! I just been thinking about coming out to see you and here y'are."

Jimmy Prescot stepped quickly out from behind the wooden counter.

"Summer, this is Jimmy," said Ryan, "proprietor of Prescot's Mercantile, best bait, tackle shop and general store on the river."

"Pleased to meet you, ma'am." Jimmy squared his shoulders. Ryan ordered hot dogs as Summer headed for the rest room to "repair" herself as she described it.

"What are you doing bringin' a woman like that out here to eat hot dogs?" whispered Jimmy when she was out of sight. "That one's a steak eater if you ask me."

"You're probably right," said Ryan. "But I'm hoping she'll acquire an appetite for catfish."

"Well now, if anybody could convince a steak eater to settle for catfish, I imagine it'ud be you." Jimmy scratched his stubbly chin. "But I wouldn't bet on it."

Ryan smiled. "It's a good thing you're not a betting man, Jimmy, you might lose on that one." He thought maybe Summer could learn to like catfish.

"Here ya' go." Jimmy set the hot dogs on the counter.

"How much do I owe you?"

"On the house," Jimmy said, waving him off. "You've done a lot for me that I'll never be able to repay."

"Forget it. How much do I owe?"

"I said, it's on the house." His tone was firm as he put a heavy hand on Ryan's shoulder. "I meant it when I said I was thinking 'bout coming to see you. I'm worried about Phoebe. Since her mother died, well, I been going through some hard times and . . . Phoebe, she's gotten real wild here lately."

"What's going on?" Ryan asked, studying the man's

worried face. It had been close to four months since Jimmy's wife, Margaret, was killed in a car accident. He knew Jimmy was taking it hard. He'd seen him in town drinking once too often to think things were anything but rocky at home.

"I can't keep an eye on Phoebe all the time," said Jimmy. "I don't know what to do. There's some older guys from Odell keep coming by. She's just sixteen. Hell, they're up to no good, I'm sure of it. Especially one of 'em. They call him Speedy. If that ain't a name for trouble, I don't know what is." He drummed his fingers on the counter. "Ya' gotta do something with her. I can't." His voice faltered.

"I'll come by tomorrow," Ryan promised, knowing it had taken a lot for Jimmy to ask for help.

Jimmy looked up at the sound of a door squeaking. The big man swiped his shirtsleeve hastily across his eyes and stepped back behind the counter as Summer eased the noisy door closed behind her.

She was composed now, her hair twisted into a neat bun and her shirttails tied tightly at her midriff. Not only did the style pull the wrinkles out, it disguised the endearingly mussed woman he'd brought in here. He was amazed at how proper she now looked.

"Would you like chili on your hot dog, miss?" asked Jimmy, his voice cheering.

"Yes, please," she said. "It smells wonderful."

"People come from miles around for my three-alarm chili," he said proudly, dipping a spoon into the crockpot he always kept going on the counter.

"Then we'll have to compare recipes, Mr. Prescot." She gave him a warm smile. "I have a four-alarm dish that'll melt spoons. Mmm, terrific," she said, sampling the chili. "What's in it?"

Ryan watched her as she listened carefully to Jimmy's recipe. He could tell she was studying the man as he recited the ingredients, and he found himself wondering if she'd overheard his emotional plea. If she had, she certainly wasn't letting on. Good. What Jimmy had just done hadn't been easy. The man would have been embarrassed to think his troubles were laid bare to a stranger.

Ryan pulled two orange sodas from the cooler and set them on the counter. "Think we can make it back to Alford by sundown?" he asked, when Jimmy and Summer moved on from discussing the merits of hamburger versus steak in chili to mustard versus ketchup in barbecue sauce.

"It's been a real pleasure," said Jimmy as he held the screen door open for them. "You come back soon, Jericho, and bring the lady." He winked, his smile looking genuine now. Ryan was glad to see the man had recovered himself, no small thanks to Summer.

They ate on the dock at Prescot's Landing, pitching pieces of hot dog bun to the ducks who'd quickly discovered an easy mark.

"So you like to cook," said Ryan above the ducks' greedy squawking.

"Oh yes. But I don't very often. I mainly collect recipes. I have a data base full. I even wrote a program that categorizes by—"

"You don't happen to have a recipe for catfish in that computer of yours, do you?" he asked hopefully.

She shook her head.

Wisps of hair that had escaped her careful ministrations floated around her face like silvery spider silk. He had a sudden urge to touch her sun-flushed cheek, to feel the warmth of her lips against his.

"Do you have one?"

"One what?"

"Catfish recipe," she whispered.

He found himself drifting into her soft green gaze. "Several." If he had any brains at all, he'd keep his distance. He leaned toward her.

"Ah, it must be getting late," she said as if waking from a daze. "Maybe we'd better be getting back."

He blinked. "It won't take us long." He crumbled the last bit of bread, allowing it to sift through his fingers. "The current will do most of the work for us."

"Do you mind if I paddle back?" she asked, her voice shaky.

"You sure you can handle it? There are a lot of switchbacks and—"

"Recent experience to the contrary, I can handle a canoe, honest." She smiled sheepishly.

He let his hands linger longer than necessary as he helped her into the canoe. It was difficult holding back, but he read enough in the signals she'd given that if he was going to have any chance at all, he'd have to go slow, let her think she was making the decisions.

"This place looks familiar," said Summer, as she stepped into the stern. "I know I haven't ever been here before." She held on to the edge of the dock while he stepped in and sat down facing her.

He propped his legs across the gunwale. "Jimmy's daughter, Phoebe, did a watercolor from the end of this dock. You might have seen it in my office."

"That's it then. She's captured the spirit of this area."

"Yes, Phoebe's got a lot going for her." If she doesn't blow it, he added to himself.

"She's good enough to pursue art as a career."

"Yes," he said, thinking Phoebe could use some of Summer's confidence and drive. It was unfortunate the two would never have a chance to know each other. He settled back, watching her guide the canoe expertly back and forth, following the current along its slow, winding path.

"Not bad," he said after she negotiated a particularly narrow bend.

She smiled, chin tilted upward. "I really was a Girl Scout."

He could certainly picture her as a determined little Girl Scout. She looked like she was used to doing what she set out to do. He stretched his legs and laced his fingers together behind his back to make a headrest. "It's nice having someone take over for a while."

"Anytime," she said companionably.

He squinted against the sun, taking in her curving outline as a feeling of contentment eased through his body. It was a sensation he hadn't had the pleasure of experiencing in a long time.

Marcus was waiting for them when they glided up to the dock at Alford Place.

"Gotta call in for Ms. Keeton 'bout an hour ago. Sounded important," he said, steadying the canoe with one hand and helping Summer out with the other. "A Mr. Maxwell Pelion from Atlanta. Wants you to call him right away. Didn't know when to tell him you'd be back." At this last comment he shifted his gaze to Ryan, giving him a wry smile.

"I hadn't intended to be gone so long," said Summer. She handed Marcus the paddle, suddenly all business. "He probably tried to get me at the clinic. What time did he call?"

Marcus shrugged. "Not too long ago."

Ryan found himself clenching his teeth. Something happened to her when Maxwell Pelion's name was mentioned. She was more skillful at composing herself than anyone he'd met in all his thirty-two years, but he'd seen it anyway. And it made him wonder.

"Would it bother Maxwell to know you hadn't spent today at your computer?" he asked, watching her eyes for an answer. The flicker of shadow was unmistakable. "Does your boss always check up on you?"

"He isn't my boss," she said. "We're partners—equal partners." Her eyes were flashing danger signals now.

Ryan ignored them. "I see," he said. "Is Maxwell the one who keeps you on that tight schedule of yours?"

"No. Max doesn't know a thing about scheduling a system installation." Her chin raised a quarter inch higher. "I take care of that end of the business."

"Just how close do you and Max work on these projects?"

"Close enough. We're business partners. I told you that." She smoothed her hair back and looked away from him.

The action gave him the uncanny feeling she'd just

slammed a door in his face. Fine, he'd just have to keep knocking. "This Maxwell, does he ever—?"

"I'd better call him back—"

"Oh? And report what you've been doing all afternoon," he said, wanting to needle her. "Would you like me to assure him you were with a customer?"

"That won't be necessary."

"But if he's keeping tabs on you, I want him to know—"

"He's not keeping tabs." She glared at him. "I may not even call him back right away."

"Suit yourself," he sighed. He hadn't even been thinking about what a call to Max would do to his delaying tactics.

"I wish you'd—" She bit her lip and then took a deep breath. "I had a nice time today, Ryan," she said, her voice controlled. "Thank you."

"Want to go again tomorrow?"

"No. That is, I'll be working at the clinic."

"I'm glad you came with me today," he said, catching her hand as she turned to go. "Don't forget, Summer, I have some catfish recipes for you." His lips brushed her cheek, and he released her quickly, not giving her the chance to pull away.

She nodded, and he watched in silence as she scurried up the path like a spooked rabbit.

"Well? What are you grinning at?" he asked Marcus who was squatting beside the canoe, holding it next to the dock.

"I can count the number of times I've seen you smile this past year on one hand," said Marcus. "And half those are from today."

Ryan sighed as he lowered himself down beside his old friend. "Has it been that bad?"

"Close to it. Not that I blame you, the circumstances bein' what they were. Seems like Ms. Keeton will do you some good."

"I don't know, Marcus." He took a deep breath. "One thing's for certain, I'm not going to be doing her any good."

FIVE

Summer rubbed her eyes and stared at the flickering computer screen. *It's still early*, she thought, *with a little luck I might get caught up by midnight.* The flicker blurred to a greenish haze. All right, it would take more than a little luck.

Long days weren't unusual at a new site, but having so little to show for them was. And it was all because her attention kept drifting, like the slow, sure swamp currents, back to Ryan Jericho. She'd expected one late night at the clinic to put her back on schedule. But that was two days ago and she'd be real lucky if it didn't take two more.

When she finally did call Max, she'd assured him everything was going perfectly—and it was, or would be. If his plans came through, she'd be on her way across the Atlantic after the Sandy Flats project was through. It left her no leeway. She wasn't going to worry Max about that, though. Even with her slow progress, she was sure she'd be finished by the six-week target date.

She tilted her head from side to side, stretching to ease the ache between her shoulder blades. She couldn't afford to slack up now, there was too much to do. And Max had been so sure he could sell the system to that hospital in Bombay.

Yawning, she fought the fatigue that threatened to take over her body. She really ought to make a cup of coffee—in a minute. Closing her eyes, she rested her forehead against the computer screen, her mind drifting along under a sunlit canopy of broad green leaves . . .

"What is this? Programming by osmosis?"

"Hummm?" she murmured, gazing up groggily.

Ryan stood in the doorway of her tiny makeshift office, his thumbs hooked into faded jeans. He was looking at her with that crooked grin that made a place in the pit of her stomach go soft.

"I–I was resting my eyes," she stammered, taking a deep breath and leaning back in her chair.

"How much longer are you going to be at this?" he asked, his tone gently accusing.

"At what? Oh, this." She adjusted the screen that had tilted down with her weight. "Another few hours at least. I need to finish configuring the—"

"You don't let up much, do you?" He frowned, a lock of dark hair falling haphazardly across his forehead.

"I have a lot to do." She didn't need this kind of distraction tonight. But when she looked into Ryan's eyes, her whole world slowed down, there seemed time for everything. "I can give you a demonstration if you'd like," she said.

"I can't right now," he said, "I'm on my way to a meeting."

"Oh." She felt a surprising pang of disappointment. "Maybe another time then. You did promise to sit through a demo. Remember?"

He grinned lazily and leaned over her computer, resting his chin on his crossed arms. "Yes, I remember. Hadn't I just been knocked senseless at the time?"

A warm tingle began to spread slowly through her body. She scooted her chair backward to stop it. "I'll probably still be here if you're free after your meeting," she said before she could stop herself.

"That might be late." He gave her a long considered look.

"I'm sure I'll be here," she said, drawing a quick breath, trying to rescue her concentration.

"Summer, you are definitely a workaholic," he said, shaking his head, his beguiling smile winning her complete attention. "You know, we do have treatments for people with problems like yours."

"Like what?"

"They're called vacations," he said, winking.

"Very funny."

His eyes twinkled, crystalline blue, making her stomach tighten.

"I'll be back at nine for that demo."

"Prepare to be impressed," she called after him, and then wished she hadn't sounded so eager.

At 9:45 she drummed her fingers impatiently on the top of the computer. She stacked her manuals, then unstacked them. She flipped through her file of diskettes, trying to decide whether or not to attempt another configuration. The last one had been disastrous. No, she wouldn't try it again, it was impossible to work when her mind wandered like this.

She'd done little more than stare at her computer for the past hour. Ryan Jericho's image replaced her screen every time she tried to enter a command.

First, his funny grin had appeared, like the Cheshire cat's, taunting her. Then his sun-bronzed face shifted slowly into focus, water dripping down each rugged angle. Finally, when his eyes scorched her with a promising fire, she'd bitten her lip and popped the diskette out of its drive in disgust. She wasn't accomplishing anything this way.

She shoved the plastic square roughly back into its envelope. Expecting Ryan to return at any moment had made her brain useless. Only her body seemed to rally. She wasn't sleepy anymore, for all the good it did her.

She stood up and paced across the small office space. How could she let this man disrupt her thinking so much? She certainly couldn't let herself get involved with him.

Humantec comes first, she told herself, taking two steps and turning. You have a job to do. Max is counting on you. This is business. She took a few more steps and whirled around again. Relationships aren't for you. Remember? You tried that already. Stick with your computers. What she was feeling for Ryan Jericho right now was . . . was hormonally induced. Chemicals, that's all. She couldn't allow mere physiology to disrupt an important project like this one.

Exasperated, and no closer to calming down, she smoothed her rumpled gray skirt, patted her bun, and marched out of her office. Dr. Ryan Jericho simply wasn't going to ruin a full night's work for her. If he didn't plan to come back, she wanted to know it. Then she could clear her mind of him and get back to business.

Except for the click of her heels on linoleum, the building was quiet as she peered down the dark hallways. After a few minutes of winding her way through the clinic's maze of corridors, she began to have second thoughts. Why should she go chasing Ryan? Why couldn't she just ignore the stupid things her body did when he was around? He probably forgot all about the demo, she told herself. He probably left after his meeting. Good, she insisted, even as her shoulders sagged.

Voices echoed toward her. Was it a woman? Yes. And more than a little upset, too, Summer judged from the strained tone, although she was too far away to make out the words.

When a lone slash of light streaked from the open door at the end of the corridor, Summer eased quietly closer. Another voice expressed the same distress. This one cracked, as a young man's would. Uncertainty froze her footsteps. Then she heard a low, unmistakably soothing voice—Ryan's. She listened, reluctant to move for fear of disturbing the clearly intense exchange.

She had meant to turn around and leave. It was obvious Ryan was with some of his clients, and their problems were none of her business. But her feet ignored her intentions, as she plastered her body against the wall outside Ryan's office.

"Phoebe, your father is not controlling your actions, you are." Ryan's voice sounded matter-of-fact, not at all cajoling. But it seemed to help the girl.

"I know . . . it's just that I . . . I can't stay there at the house. It's horrible, he yells and . . ." There was a soft sound of weeping.

"My folks are only interested in rules too. If I break them a few times, they act like they'll hate me forever," another added. Other voices mumbled assent.

"It's rough when you feel that those you love can't handle what you've gotten yourself into." More agreement.

"But the choice is yours. You can run away, or you can find ways to cope," Ryan continued his straightforward approach.

"Yeah, but . . ."

Summer leaned against the wall, knowing she shouldn't listen but captivated by his careful responses. He knew just how to challenge, yet support at the same time.

She tried to slip back into the shadows when a young pale-haired girl stepped out of the office. Sad brown eyes stared at her in surprise.

"Excuse me," said Summer, straightening her back and moving into the light, "I was . . . waiting for Dr. Jericho."

"Summer?" It was Ryan.

"I was wondering where you were and—"

"Who is she?" asked the girl in a small but accusing voice.

"Summer Keeton, computer wizard and canoer extraordinaire," said Ryan, smiling broadly. "Summer, this is my friend Phoebe Prescot." He tugged the girl's hair playfully, and she gave him a quick smile that died almost as soon as it was born.

"Hi," said Phoebe as she eyed Summer with clear suspicion.

"Hello, Phoebe," she said, using her most encouraging look. So this is Jimmy's daughter. She'd been careful not to reveal to Ryan what she'd heard. Poor girl, she knew what it was like to lose a mother. No one else can love you in quite the same, selfless way. "It's so nice to meet you," she said.

"I've got to go," said Phoebe abruptly.

Ryan gave Phoebe's shoulder a kindly squeeze. "See you next time," he said.

"Right." The girl nodded.

Summer recognized the tone he'd used with the girl, soft, but infinitely persuasive.

"I'm sorry, I didn't mean to interrupt," said Summer, as the last of the small group of teenagers left. "I thought maybe you'd forgotten about the demo."

"The session ran late. I should have warned you that sometimes that happens." He shrugged in apology.

"No problem," she said brightly, determined not to seem disappointed.

He propped his hand against the wall beside her head. "How long will this demonstration of yours take?" he asked, his face close to hers—too close.

She took a deep breath. "I'd like to show you the whole package. It'll only take an hour or so . . ."

"That long?"

"To do it justice."

His fingertips feathered across her jaw. She took another breath.

"I usually go through the office automation software first," she said, "but the best part is the data base module. That's all mine. Maybe we could—"

"Reschedule." His hand stilled. "You look like you need a break."

She turned her face away. "Of course. It is late." She managed to keep the tremble out of her voice. "I forget most people don't keep long hours like I do." She inched away from him, just far enough to control her heartbeat.

"Oh, I can keep long hours when I need to," he said, grinning. "Have you had dinner?"

"Er . . . yes."

He rolled his eyes. "Let me guess. A pack of crackers from the machine."

"Cheese puffs, actually."

"That isn't a meal. I'm starving and I know a perfect spot on the river, come with me."

"I really can't. I'm—"

"You're working, I know. How about a compromise? While we eat, you can give me the same spiel you would if I was watching the demo."

"But it's not the same—"

"C'mon. You need a decent meal, and a break. This way you get both, and can still talk about your system." He took her hands, enclosing them in his strong grip. "The only logical thing to do is say yes."

She felt the warmth of his fingers spread up her arm. "Well, I suppose . . ." Her mind blanked as the glowing sensation grew until it covered her whole body.

"You suppose what?" he whispered, drawing her to him with a slow, irresistible force.

"I suppose I could cut the day a little short. That is, only if we discuss Humantec." She felt his hands splay across her back.

"I think we can manage that," he said, lowering his lips to hers.

Her thoughts blurred into the warmth of his deepening kiss. A small fire started in the core of her being and then grew, spreading its tendrils hungrily throughout her body. She pulled away, too stunned to wonder at its unexpected force.

"Wh–Where are we going?" she stammered.

He chuckled deep and low. "I'm not quite sure, Summer. Where *are* we going?"

"For dinner, I mean." She stepped back, shaken.

He took her hand, halting her retreat. "Oh yes, that. A nice, private place on the river."

"Prescot's?"

"No, the place I have in mind is a little more secluded." His warm smile slowed her tremble. "Although I'm sure Jimmy would welcome you to dinner anytime."

Summer swished her feet through the cool water. "It's enchanting," she said, bracing her hands on the rough wooden dock, looking up at the house. Built on stilts, it jutted out over the water like a bird ready to pounce.

"This is the perfect spot," she said dreamily. "You built this little cottage yourself?"

"Little cottage? Aunt Carrie calls it a hovel."

She giggled. "It needs a little work," she said, looking up the stairway that led from the dock to a partially finished screened porch, "but it's definitely not a hovel."

"Alford Place is only a few miles upstream from here. We'll come this way in the canoe someday."

"Next time with two paddles, I hope," she said. No, there shouldn't even be a next time. She shouldn't waste another day, especially in this swamp. What was happening to her? She resisted her mind's urge to drift. Whatever it was, being here made it worse. The swamp had a way of slowing her down, soothing her, so that she no longer felt the urgency of time. The concept of maintaining a schedule seemed ludicrous here.

Ryan cocked his head. "Our first excursion didn't turn out too terribly bad, now did it?"

"Oh . . . ah, no. I guess it didn't." She swallowed hard. "But I think I should be well armed when I'm around you."

"I see, well armed at all times," he said wryly.

"Of course," she attempted a stern look only to have it melt under his amused gaze. To block the giddy feeling that nudged at her insides, she picked up another slice of pizza. "Do you want this last—?"

A mournful howl filled the swamp, halting her in midsentence. It started low and built steadily until it ended in a spine-tingling series of high-pitched yaps.

She dropped the pizza back into its box. "What is it?" she asked, scooting closer to Ryan who obligingly wrapped his arms around her.

"Swamp Monster," he said in a solemn voice.

"Of course." She allowed herself to snicker, but only because he was holding her so securely. The eerie sound welled up out of the night mist once again, closer this time. She shivered at the strange wail echoing around them.

After a few moments, moments in which Summer's

attention shifted from the strange sound to the warm, strong arms around her, Ryan gave a short whistle and the howling stopped.

"Obedient monster," she said, pulling out of his embrace before the sensations tingling throughout her body made her heart race out of control.

"Swamp Monster is a dog," he said. "He wandered out of the swamp one day and has been with me ever since. Thinks I need company, I guess."

"Why won't he come out now?"

"Because you're here. He doesn't trust people very easily. But when he does, I think it's forever." He studied her, his unsettling blue gaze forcing her to turn away.

She put her fingers to her lips and whistled, amazed that the dryness in her mouth let a sound escape.

A questioning whine answered.

Ryan added a low, "Here, boy, c'mon," and a large brown-and-black brindled dog crept out of the bushes at the water's edge.

"I can see why you call him Swamp Monster," Summer said as the shaggy creature watched her curiously. "Hey, Monster. Good dog. Want some pizza?" She waved the last piece of pizza at him.

"Hold on," said Ryan. "If you're not going to eat it, I will."

"You hold on, I'm making friends now. Don't interrupt." Tantalizing the dog with a bit of pepperoni, she coaxed him to her, calling his name in low, soothing tones.

"I don't believe it," said Ryan as the dog trotted toward them, sniffed at her, and took the pepperoni she held out. "I knew he'd be interested, food's always on his mind. But to actually take it from a stranger's hand . . ."

A short while later, Summer sat stroking Swamp Monster while his head lolled on her lap in helpless adoration. The dog had not only eaten the pizza, but was lying comfortably on the dock between her and Ryan.

"So you've widened your select circle of friends," said Ryan, eyeing his dog, "I think I'm jealous." Monster looked up at him and thumped his tail on the dock, but made no move to vacate his position.

"It's a full moon," said Ryan. "Nice night for catfishing. We could take the boat." He pointed to an ancient but well-kept fishing boat moored on the opposite side of the dock. The current caused it to bump softly against the tire strips nailed to the pilings.

Summer hesitated, and then felt the dog nose her hand, as if demanding a response for its master. "Weren't we supposed to talk about Humantec?" she said quickly, scratching behind Monster's floppy ears.

"Ah yes, Humantec." The angles of Ryan's face hardened.

"You did promise to hear about that demo. I mean, that's why I came out here."

"Is it?"

"Yes." She cleared her throat. "Why are you so against our computers?" she asked.

"I'm not. It's a matter of priorities." He rubbed his chin and cocked his head to one side, his eyes brightening. "C'mon, let's go for a walk."

He grabbed both her hands and pulled her up before she could protest. Monster stretched, looking mildly disgruntled at being disturbed. Groaning loudly, he ambled away.

The sandy path along the river was washed in silvery moonlight, making it easy to follow. "You met Phoebe Prescot tonight," said Ryan.

"Her eyes were so sad," Summer said, wondering how Jimmy could be so certain Ryan could help. She'd been too uncomfortable about it to tell Ryan she'd overheard their conversation that day in the store. She looked up at the man walking beside her. What did it take to instill that kind of faith in someone?

"Phoebe's been through some rough times—so have the other kids." His gaze followed the dark river, and he seemed to forget her for a moment. "These aren't your usual disgruntled adolescents," he said. "They've stepped over that line long before I ever see them." Picking up a pebble, he threw it at a cypress tree that rose out of the water a few yards away, hitting it dead on. The thud echoed around them.

"Some of the kids who end up at our clinic have alienated just about anyone who has ever cared about them. Their support systems are in shambles, and it's up to us to help rebuild that." He looked at her, his shadowed face grim. "And there are those out there, like Phoebe, whose families have simply fallen apart."

"I know that, Ryan—"

"Even where there's a lot of love, volatile emotions need time and space to diffuse." He paused.

She could hear his breathing, a long intake, and a slow, wavering exhale. She wondered how he could help someone like Phoebe. It was an impossible task. You couldn't fight the pain of losing a family, she knew that much. You had to bury it as deep as you could dig. Phoebe would learn—it was the only way.

"The clinic was going to open a halfway house," said Ryan, his voice bringing her back with a jolt. "But that was before Humantec launched its assault on Sandy Flats." His jaw worked. "Now we have a bunch of slick computers and no place for the kids," he said tightly.

Summer licked her drying lips. She'd come to Humantec's defense hundreds of times, but it seemed harder tonight than ever before. "But, Ryan, Humantec is in this business to help people, just like you are. I assure you, the productivity increase will save Sandy Flats enough money in the long run to—"

Even in the shadows of the moon, she could see Ryan's smoldering glare. She hesitated, then plowed on, wanting desperately to convince him that Humantec wasn't responsible for his problem.

She quoted her usual statistics, but they sounded hard and cold even to her own ears. They were just empty numbers compared to the needs of the children he'd just described.

Ryan touched her softly on the shoulder. "Who is this talking?" he asked, his hand sliding slowly down her arm.

"Me, Summer," she said, her thoughts dissolving in confusion.

"Summer, the Humantec computer wiz, or Summer, the woman who, for a brief moment, was interested in what Humantec is doing to help people like Phoebe."

"Ryan, Humantec didn't make the decision to take

away your money. I'm just here to do a job. This is business."

"Business. That explains it." He shook his head.

She felt cold even though the night was warm. "There are other places in the state to send your clients besides your halfway house," she said, compelled to defend Humantec's position, her position.

He leaned against the low-hanging limb of an ancient oak and tugged at a wisp of Spanish moss. "It's difficult enough to convince a father to let his child leave home," he said. "A few hundred miles makes a lot of difference."

"I'm sorry the house wasn't funded," she said, watching him crumble the moss. She fought the urge to apologize any further. She'd designed a good system. It was supposed to help people. She wasn't responsible for the way her project was funded. "In all the years we've been marketing this system, we've had nothing but positive results," she said, the words drifting past him like dead leaves on a fall day.

He studied her with piercing intensity. "Sandy Flats can't afford to invest in technology over people," he said, after a long pause. His eyes darkened. "Summer, there's something you need to know, I will do everything I can to stop your project."

"But, Ryan, you can't stop it." It took a lot to break an agreement with Humantec, and it wasn't at all likely he'd succeed, not with Max Pelion to deal with. "We have a binding contract with the clinic," she said, her voice firm. Surely he didn't think she would just quit and go home? "It's not as bad as you think. We've worked with other clinics just like this one. Humantec is here to help." The words sounded too smooth, but what else could she say?

He remained silent, staring at her, jaw set, eyes icy blue, but a sadness in them she hadn't seen before. Regret? She made herself look away before she could begin to wonder.

"You can't expect me to back off now," she said, watching the water shimmer in the moonlight.

"Back off? No, Summer, I don't expect that. Not of you." She heard him move toward her.

"Then what do you expect?" she asked, her smooth veneer thinning with each of his footsteps.

"I wanted you to understand," he said quietly.

"I see."

"Do you? I'm fighting Humantec, not you."

She flinched as he touched her arm.

Willing her trigger-happy muscles to relax, she turned to him, wearing her coolest professional smile. "I'm here as Humantec's representative," she said evenly. "It isn't possible to separate my—"

"Summer, Humantec is a company—you are not." Her smile faltered as he put his hands on her shoulders and began to knead the stiffness from them with warm, strong fingers. "Summer, dear lady, I don't want to fight you," he whispered, pulling her close. "I don't give a damn about Humantec—but I do care about you."

His lips lowered to hers, salty, pliant, tantalizing. She could do nothing but allow his exploration. His arms tightened and her lips melted against his, her questions swimming helplessly in a surge of sensation. She knew she should go somewhere and bolt the door.

He made her feel so confused. Only her body seemed to know how to respond.

Ryan's hands slid in sensuous arcs down her back, igniting fires wherever she felt their warmth. Slowly they circled her waist and then trailed down farther. Just as she was certain her mind would drown in the urgency taking control of her body, a hard, cold thought crept through the yearnings of her senses. Was this what he meant by doing everything he could to stop her? Fear wrapped its fingers around the slow quiver of her heart, and still, she couldn't move.

"Ryan . . . I . . . we can't." Summer tried to steady the rapid beating of her heart. "I am not going to stop the project, if that's what this is all about."

His hands froze on her hips, and he looked at her as if she'd spoken in some foreign tongue. Then he let out a long, slow exhale.

She stepped back, fighting to clear her mind. "I'm Humantec's representative. And I will defend its interests to the last."

"This isn't a war," he said, his voice husky.

"I'm going to do my job. A contract is a contract, and I'm already installing the system. All you're doing is making it difficult for everyone."

He shoved his fingers through his hair. "You're right about that," he said tightly.

Summer frowned at her reflection in the bedroom mirror. The morning light revealed dark circles beneath her eyes, telltale signs of how she'd slept. She picked up her brush and pulled it through her curls. Every movement seemed to take forever, as if she were still asleep. She'd been this way for the better part of a week—since she'd last seen Ryan.

She couldn't deny that he'd awakened something inside her. Something she hadn't known existed. No one had ever made her feel the way he did when his hands had played over her body. Certainly not Max. And no one had so completely occupied her thoughts in his absence.

She shuddered, and yanked the brush mercilessly through a tangle. There was simply a strange kind of chemistry between them. That would explain it. Her feelings for Ryan Jericho were chemical and nothing more. Yes, that was it. She would just have to stay away from him. Eventually she'd forget and then she could continue with her work as usual. And never, ever could she let him touch her again.

Her hand went to her hip involuntarily, to the place he'd last touched her. She felt herself flush, the sensation heating her skin. Oh yes, she did have to stay away from him. Humantec was her only priority. It was her life. Her solid, predictable life.

Tossing the brush on the dresser, she pulled her hair back and began the troublesome task of twisting it into a bun. She wouldn't let Max or herself down, not now, not when they were so close to their dream. A curl escaped her gold barrette and drooped irritatingly over her face. Their dream? It used to seem so right, so reasonable.

A light tap sounded at the bedroom door.

"Summer, oh, Summer, are you in there?" Carrie Alford called to her in a birdlike voice. "Dearest, I need your help. It's . . . It's urgent."

"Come in," said Summer, unclasping the barrette and tossing it onto the table.

Carrie peeked around the door, her lip quivering. "I promised to chaperon a trip to the beach for a group from Sandy Flats," she said. "And now the garden club is meeting and I can't possibly go. I don't know what to do. Oh dear, just say you'll help me." Her face twisted, tiny tears forming in the corners of her eyes.

"Please don't cry, Carrie." Summer quickly pulled out a tissue. Tears unnerved her. Her own came only when she peeled onions. "What can I do?" she asked, hoping the problem was something small, something easily corrected. This wasn't a day she felt up to dealing with anything.

"You'll help then?" said Carrie.

"Of course, yes. What?"

"Oh, thank you. This is wonderful! I'll go tell them! Hurry up, dear, they're almost ready to leave." She darted out.

"Wait!"

Carrie peeked her head back around the door, looking oddly sheepish.

"What am I supposed to do?" asked Summer.

"Just go with the children to the beach today. Everything's been arranged. It's a coed group, so we have to have one male and one female chaperon." Carrie fluffed her hair. "All you have to do is go along and be female." Her eyes twinkled.

"But I was on my way to work and I—"

"Oh my, on a Saturday. I had no idea you'd be going in today. Dear, dear . . ." Carrie held the now-wadded tissue up to her face. "Wh . . . What'll I do. I can't go downstairs and tell them they can't go. Those children will be devastated," she said, her chin beginning to quiver.

"Don't cry. Please." Summer swallowed hard. "I'll go."

"I knew I could count on you!" Carrie sniffed, and dabbed her eyes, recovering remarkably fast. "Bless you, Summer girl," she said. "Now, do you have a bathing suit with you?"

"No. But—"

"No matter. I can take care of that. Hurry now." She was gone.

How difficult could a day at the beach with little children be? She'd come back and put in a long night at the clinic. That would work, she guessed.

Summer pulled on her plain white T-shirt and climbed into the only pair of shorts she'd brought. Not much you can do about it now, she thought, running her hands over the faded denim. There just weren't many casual clothes in her wardrobe. She pulled a string from the fringe where she'd cut them off and frowned.

"You should wear shorts more often," said Carrie, whirling back into the room and tossing a straw bag onto the bed. "They make you look—"

"Sloppy?"

"Relaxed is the word I was looking for," she said, her blue gaze appraising. "You are lovely."

"Thanks," said Summer, wincing at the compliment, the look Carrie was leveling at her as mesmerizing as any Ryan had ever used.

She shook the thought aside. Sloppy was how she felt, downright disheveled, through and through. She never needed anything other than work clothes when she traveled. It was lucky she'd thrown in the old jeans and T-shirt, thinking they'd be comfortable to wear when she was alone in her hotel room. This trip was not going at all as expected.

"Look, dear." Carrie pulled a floppy hat and a jewel-green bathing suit from the bag. "You can't go to the beach without these."

Summer took the hat, but her smile faltered as Carrie spread the skimpily cut suit on the bed.

"It belonged to my niece, Alicia. Take it, please. She never wore it."

Summer fingered the soft material, it definitely wasn't the basic-black-cover-everything she was used to.

"You're taller than Alicia, but slimmer," said Carrie, her gaze traveling over Summer's narrow hips. "Come child, they'll be leaving any minute. You'll look fine in it."

"I don't suppose I have much choice. Are you sure Alicia won't mind?"

Carrie paused and touched her fingers to her lips. "Don't see how she could. She passed away last fall."

"Oh." Summer struggled to remember what Ryan had said about her. How could she have missed that? "I'm sorry. Ryan mentioned his sister, but I didn't—"

"He doesn't talk about it much." Carrie sighed, shaking her head.

Summer could see the memory was a painful one and was about to change the subject when Carrie eased her tiny form down on the bed, her weight barely denting the neatly tucked spread.

"From the time Ryan and Alicia were just little things, they were so close," said Carrie, lowering her voice as she smoothed the suit flat and began to fold it slowly. "Alicia was a lot like her mother—vulnerable somehow, the perennial child. But she didn't have parents that were there to take care of her—only Ryan. He was always trying to protect her—not that she made it easy for him, mind you. Poor kids." Putting the suit back into the bag, she sighed softly, gazing out the window to the garden beyond.

"My sister and her husband sent them to the best schools, bought them anything they wanted. Oh, they owned so much, but it meant so little. All they really had was each other. Dear Ry boy," she said, wistfully. "He wants to take care of everybody—such an impossible task."

Summer felt the love in the woman's voice and pictured Ryan as a young boy, trying to fill a man's shoes. His rough edges made better sense to her now. Ryan, too, had had his heartaches.

"Look at us," Carrie said, standing up and brushing off her dress as if to be rid of the sadness. She patted Summer's cheek and smiled. "Heavens, I've rattled on too much." She turned as she reached the door, hesitating. "Summer love, trust me, whatever happens, I know you were guided to this house for a reason."

"What do you mean?" asked Summer, suddenly uncomfortable.

"Ah, child, you'll understand soon enough," she whispered, a fierce certainty glowing in her eyes.

Summer smiled, nodding hypnotically in agreement while still puzzling over the conviction in Carrie's wizened face. Trying to understand the woman was like squinting through shifting mist.

"Oh, I do hope Marcus has everything ready," Carrie said, fluttering out the door.

"I appreciate your help with the bathing suit."

"It was nothing, sweet. Do you need anything else?"

"No," said Summer, picking up her barrette and preparing to do battle with her hair again. "I'm fine, but who else is going on this excursion?"

"La, didn't I tell you? It's Ryan and his group."

Her hand slipped, and the barrette fell with a loud clatter.

"Such lovely locks," said Carrie as she looped her arm through Summer's and guided her out the door. "You are perfectly beautiful."

A loud group of teenagers greeted her in the front hall.

"Terrific, you're coming!" called Ryan over the heads of the youngsters chattering all around him. "I was beginning to wonder if I'd have to call this trip off."

She started to scowl at him but noticed Phoebe standing just inside the door, the only one not adding to the unsettling din. She ignored Ryan and wound her way toward the girl.

"Joel, can you help Marcus with that cooler?" called Ryan, motioning to a boy who was playfully snapping his towel at anyone who was unmindful enough to come within his reach. "Phoebe, how about grabbing these picnic baskets for me?"

Phoebe abandoned her position by the door and was replaced by Ryan. Summer immediately veered off her original course.

"Here, dear," said Carrie, slipping through the

crowd to her side. "You'll need extra towels, I'm sure."
She shoved a tall stack of floral-print towels into Summer's arms. Holding her chin at the top of the stack,
Summer tried to keep from dropping the straw bag
dangling from her shoulder as Carrie plopped the
floppy hat on her head and gently shoved her out the
front door with the rest of the group.

"I hope you don't mind. I appreciate you doing
this," said Ryan when she stopped to stare at the dilapidated bus parked in the drive. With her chin tilted up
at such an awkward angle by the towels, all she could
manage was, "Hmm."

He turned to Marcus who was supervising the loading of the cooler. "How many sodas have we packed?"

"Plenty. Got lots of ice too. It's gonna be a hot
one," said Marcus. The youngsters were boarding the
bus, shouting and jostling each other, sounding as if
they were a crowd of a hundred instead of twelve.

Ryan winked at Summer. "Are we ready?"

"Hmm," she mumbled again and started down the
steps.

"Let me take that, you can't see a thing." He lifted
the towels from her arms and smiled broadly.

She stared at the bus, then at Ryan. He looked totally appealing in his black polo shirt and khaki shorts.

"Thank you for being such a good sport about
this," he said softly. She grit her teeth when her heartbeat quickened, and she purposely shifted her gaze back
toward the bus. "Is this your doing, Ryan Jericho?"

"Carrie is usually very reliable."

She shot him a quick glance.

His face beamed pure innocence. "I don't know

how she got her dates confused. But that garden club of hers, you can imagine—"

"Ryan, I don't think this is a good—"

He touched her shoulder, gently pulling her around to face him. "Please. Come with us for one day, that's all I'm asking."

"When Carrie asked me, I didn't expect—"

"C'mon, lady. What's the harm in it?"

Eyeing the bus, she adjusted her hat, holding tight to the bag under her arm. She should turn around right now. She had better things to do today than baby-sit problem children.

When she opened her mouth to give him a resounding "Forget it!" the words died in her throat. Phoebe was watching intently from her seat, alone in the back of the bus. Summer looked at Ryan. His expression told her he'd already registered her change of heart.

She shrugged his hand from her shoulder. "I must be crazy," she said, stepping off the porch.

SIX

The bathing suit fit like no other suit Summer had ever worn, making her feel sensual and slightly wicked. She pulled her T-shirt back on over it.

Phoebe, who was standing behind her in the cramped shower house, giggled. "No guts," she said. "Might've known."

"Guts? It's not a matter of guts, Phoebe. It's simply a matter of—"

"Of what?"

"It's a matter of propriety."

"Like I said, no guts."

Summer hesitated, detecting the challenge in Phoebe's tone. The tenuous beginnings of a friendship had formed between them during the bus ride to the beach. She didn't want to jeopardize it by seeming like a prude. It had felt good to be confided in.

When in doubt, bluff. She smiled at Phoebe and pulled off the T-shirt, stuffing it into her straw bag before she changed her mind. Turning to face Phoebe, she tried her best sexy pose, "No guts, eh?"

Phoebe snorted. "If I had a body like that, I'd sure show it off."

Summer put on her hat with a flourish and grabbed her bag, slinging it over her shoulder. "Do you need any help with those?" she asked as Phoebe struggled with a huge sketch pad under one arm, an easel under the other, and a canvas bag dangling precariously from her shoulder.

"Thanks," said Phoebe, handing her the sketch pad. "I haven't been able to paint in a while. Dad's been making me work at the store—so he can keep an eye on me, he says." She shook her head. "He thinks he can keep me away from my boyfriend by making me stay at the store all the time," she said. "He just doesn't understand anything." She picked up her easel and wrestled it out the narrow door.

"He sounds a bit like my father," said Summer companionably.

Phoebe shrugged. "No one could be as bad as Daddy. His list of rules would overload a landfill in no time."

Summer chuckled. "Same with my father. His regulations came straight from marine boot camp."

Phoebe wrinkled her nose. "You're kidding."

"It was the best he could do after Mom died. I don't think he was quite prepared to raise a daughter."

"Did he question every move you made, and accuse you of things you hadn't even thought of doing?"

Summer adjusted the sketch pad under her arm. "Phoebe, maybe your father needs time to get used to the idea that he's your only parent now."

"So what do I do in the meantime?"

"I pretty much kept my chin up, my eyes down, and my mouth shut."

Phoebe let out a snort.

"You asked," said Summer. "I'm just telling you what worked for me."

"Well, I'm no marine."

"I can see that." Summer rested a hand on the girl's shoulder. "I know it's hard, but I also know you'll live through this."

Phoebe smiled tentatively.

"For today at least, you get to do something you enjoy," Summer said, determined to keep that smile in place. "So where's the best place to paint from around here?"

"The dunes."

"We ought to have a good view of the beach there."

"Yes. And anything else that might happen by," said Phoebe suggestively.

They both laughed. It was a comfortable sound. As they followed the sandy path that wound toward the ocean she decided the day wasn't going to turn out so bad after all.

"Hello, ladies," said Ryan, catching a wildly thrown Frisbee before it beaned her. He gave Phoebe a hug and Summer an appreciative grin.

Instinctively, she shifted the large pad of paper around to rest strategically in front of her.

"We've got the volleyball net set up out on the beach. Are you ready for a game?" he asked, not taking his eyes away from the paper that fluttered in the ocean breeze.

"I don't think so," said Summer. Her skin heated at the thought, and she hoped he wouldn't push the idea.

She wasn't about to bounce around in this bathing suit after a volleyball, not in front of those keen eyes of Ryan's. They didn't miss anything.

"You two aren't going to run off by yourselves all day, are you?" His frown showed disappointment, but his eyes twinkled.

"Phoebe was going to paint a beach scene from up on the dunes. We were just talking about the perfect view she'd have from there."

Phoebe nodded, grinning slowly.

Ryan folded his arms across his chest and then rubbed his chin.

For a moment, Summer was afraid he was going to persist. But he surprised her.

"I see," he said, flicking Phoebe's hair out of her eyes. "Enjoy yourself, kiddo," he said softly. "And you, Summer. Don't forget, you're the chaperon. Watch this kid carefully. Don't let her eat any sand or—"

"Dr. Jericho," said Phoebe. Her tone was exasperated, but she was looking up at Ryan with adoration in her eyes.

Ryan won everyone's heart, thought Summer. He knew what each person responded to and could put them at ease or frighten them to death at his own whim.

He winked at Summer, and she realized she'd been staring. It wasn't just his broad chest and well-defined muscles that were holding her attention so thoroughly. She simply enjoyed watching him with the group of teenagers that had surrounded him. It was obvious to her, counseling was the absolute perfect job for Ryan Jericho.

❖————————❖

As Ryan waded out of the surf, he noticed Summer, still standing at the top of the sand dune where Phoebe sat with her easel. It was the first time he'd gotten a full view of those beautiful, long legs. He lifted his hand, she waved. Drawing in a deep breath, he let the air's salty tang fill his lungs.

He was glad Summer had shown an interest in Phoebe. On the bus ride he'd stolen glimpses of them in the rearview mirror from the driver's seat. At first he'd been worried. Summer had been unusually quiet. He'd even wondered if he'd made a mistake bringing her. And he knew well enough how difficult Phoebe could be when she was on a stubborn streak. While Summer hadn't exactly begun the trip in the best of moods, the camaraderie growing between her and Phoebe was heartening.

He couldn't have planned it better if he'd tried. Phoebe needed a good role model—a woman who was strong-willed, intelligent, and successful. Summer Kee-ton was all of that. And a whole lot more, he thought, watching her pick her way through the dancing sea oats, holding her hat on with both hands. He waved again, and she stopped. He had a sudden fear that she might turn around and run. He motioned her to him. She might still be out of sorts about coming, but he wasn't going to let her avoid him the whole day.

She stood still for a moment, then started slowly toward him. Graceful even in the soft sand, her slender form thoroughly captivated his attention as she crossed the wide beach. Her bathing suit, a shimmer of green cut high on the sides and low everywhere else, sculpted her body perfectly. His gaze followed every liquid movement of her approach.

Behind him, a wave crashed, sending a spray of cool water across the backs of his legs. "Nice suit," he said, hoping he didn't sound as lascivious as he felt.

She smiled, not quite looking at him. "I borrowed it. I guess it doesn't fit quite like—"

"It fits fine." He swallowed hard.

"It . . . It's not exactly, ah—"

"—your style," he finished for her. He suspected his stare was making her uncomfortable but he didn't look away.

"Carrie said it would be okay to wear it," said Summer, adjusting the spaghetti straps. She took off her hat and examined the brim for a long moment. "She said the suit belonged to your sister. I hope my wearing it doesn't bother you," she said.

"No." With effort he dragged his gaze away from the long, slow curves that had parched his throat.

"Ryan"—Summer's eyes lifted to meet his, their green suddenly murky—"I didn't realize she . . . I'm very sorry."

He turned to watch the waves roll toward them and automatically counted the heads of the swimmers. What had Aunt Carrie told her? She was only supposed to help him get Summer to the beach, not discuss the family tragedies.

He looked at Summer's upturned face, wondering if she could possibly understand. "Did Aunt Carrie tell you what happened?" he asked.

"Only that Alicia had died."

There was something deep in her clear eyes when she answered him, something expectant about the tilt of her delicate chin. It was as if a door had suddenly opened.

"Alicia killed herself, last October," he said, wondering why he felt like talking about it now. But he sensed a strength in Summer's calm acceptance that girded him on. "She had been very depressed," he said quietly. "We found her after she'd slashed her wrists—a few hours too late."

He watched as she carefully composed her expression into one of sympathy or pity, he didn't know which. He wanted neither. Why had he felt the urge to tell her? She couldn't help him.

"I had no idea," she said, her voice sounding sickeningly gentle.

He didn't want her to feel sorry for him, he didn't deserve it. No, Aunt Carrie couldn't have filled in all the details for her. He'd failed Alicia, as sure as if he'd held the knife to her himself. Ryan clenched his teeth against the old horror, forcing it back to its dark hiding place.

"The suit looks very nice on you," he said, determined to leave the subject far behind.

Summer's smile was uncertain.

"Alicia's taste in clothes was outrageous," he said, making his tone light. "She wasn't one to worry about practicality, but she did know how to show off her assets."

Summer reddened.

"Don't be embarrassed. I meant that as a compliment," he said quickly. He was gratified when her faltering smile had steadied.

"Your sister must have been an interesting person."

"Oh, that she was." His laugh was bittersweet. "I

never knew what to expect. Full of fun and silliness one minute and deadly serious the next. She could fool you." He drew in a long breath, letting the warm salt air penetrate the tightness in his chest. "Strangely enough, there are things that actually seem clearer from a distance."

"I don't think that's strange at all," she said, her tone certain. "I've found it easier to handle quite a few things from a respectable distance." She put her hat on and pulled down the brim until he could no longer see her eyes.

"Trust me, Summer, you can't always watch life from the safety of the shadows," he said.

"Hey, Dr. Jericho!"

The call came from the surf, and he turned to see a tall figure wade toward him, shaking the water from red hair that spiked straight out at the sides. "You gonna finish this bodysurfing contest, or are you gonna make time?"

Ryan grinned at the boy. Joel was carrying his lanky frame with a cockiness that hadn't been there a few months ago, a far cry from the sullen kid he'd started working with. He was going to miss kids like Joel—a lot.

He flipped the brim of Summer's hat back. "Are you coming in?"

"I don't think this suit will hold up in water," she said.

"It might."

"I doubt it." She tested a strap and shook her head.

"Yo, Dr. J," said Joel, giving Summer a shy nod. "You could just concede defeat, accept the fact you're just another aging athlete, and stay here on the beach."

"I could," said Ryan.

"No you can't, Ryan. You go show 'em what an elderly man can do."

Summer smiled, and he wanted nothing more than to stand there on the beach, watching her.

"I think I'll go see how Phoebe's doing with her painting," she said.

"You coming, Jericho?" Joel called, plunging back through the breakers.

"Yes, he is," said Summer, giving him a not-so-light shove toward the water.

Ryan had always loved bodysurfing. He enjoyed matching his own rhythm to that of the sea, waiting for the right wave and catching it at just the point in its curl that would give him the maximum ride.

But he had trouble paying attention to the waves today. He'd missed more than one to seek out the dune where Summer and Phoebe sat. When he looked at her, and that was more and more often, she would shimmer slightly out of focus. He knew there was much more to her than she willingly revealed, but he couldn't get quite close enough to be certain of what it was.

He'd made a career of exploring other people's lives, working through layers of defenses with the skills he'd honed for his profession. Understanding Summer was so much different from analyzing a client.

With Phoebe Prescot, he could use any number of therapeutic techniques to get at her fears and frustrations. He could help her work toward concrete goals—goals like communicating with her father and accepting her mother's death.

But when it came to Summer, his clinical perspective was about as functional as his old fishing boat with the engine flooded.

He glanced up at the dune and felt a sensation of rightness at seeing the two women's heads bowed toward each other, Summer nodding as if in agreement. It would be nice if she could be here longer than a few weeks. He shook the water from his hair, wondering where that thought had come from. He was supposed to be trying to get rid of her. He really did need to be more objective.

"Looks like I'm outsurfing you today, Doc!" shouted Joel. "You going to wait for the perfect wave or what?"

Ryan watched Joel catch a wave and shoot past him, deciding he'd better get down to the business of surfing before he ran out of time. The wind had picked up, making the swells bigger, and a line of clouds on the horizon was beginning to clump into dark piles. He glanced once more toward shore, but this time only sea oats waved from the top of the dunes.

Feeling the pull of a large incoming swell, Ryan kicked hard until he was gliding just below the lip of the curl. The wave's force gathered around him, lifting, shoving him forward, gaining speed as it bubbled inland. With his head down and arms outstretched, he rode it, propelled like an arrow, shooting straight toward shore.

And then he felt his hands graze something where nothing should be, but it was too late to veer away, too much momentum insisting he continue forward. Instantly, he was tumbling head over heels into a mass of arms and legs.

"What the—?" Gasping for breath, he wiped the

salt sting from his eyes and caught a glimpse of brilliant green in the foam around him. Grabbing it in the swirling, waist-deep surf, he watched Summer's head pop up just as he felt something give way. She cried out, clutching at the top of her suit. Another wave hit, and she was down again.

He lunged forward, feeling his ankle twist as he reached for her. He found her arm and pulled.

"My suit," she said, fumbling with her strap. She swayed against him in the current.

He stumbled back, letting out an oath as a sliver of pain shot through his ankle.

"You're hurt," she said, steadying him. The top of her suit slipped.

He grinned.

She sank down into the water, pulling him with her.

"Here, Summer, let me—"

"No, don't."

"I'll just pull the strap this way."

"No you won't," she said quickly. "You'll have to—" The rest was drowned out by another wave.

"We can't just stay here," he said, trying to stand. He felt her arm go around his waist.

"Come on," she said, pressing against his side. She wedged herself under his arm and twisted toward him so that his side covered what her suit did not. She was warm and soft, curving deliciously into him. He felt an overwhelming urge to just settle back into the water with her.

"You've got to help," she commanded, pulling him up with surprising strength.

So she was going to be practical, was she? He should have expected that.

After considerable awkward struggle, they reached the beach, falling clumsily onto the sand. He closed his eyes, letting the water lap at his throbbing ankle. "Now what?" he asked, aware of every inch of her length along his side.

"Don't move," she said. There was steel in her voice.

"I wouldn't think of it," he answered congenially, snuggling closer.

"Okay ya'll," he heard Phoebe say somewhere above them. "Isn't it a little public out here for this sort of thing?"

"Phoebe, Dr. Jericho has hurt his ankle and my bathing suit's torn," said Summer, matter-of-factly. "Could you get us some towels?"

"Oh sure," said Phoebe. Ryan opened one eye and watched her pad along the hard-packed sand up the beach.

Summer moved a little beside him, and he opened both of his eyes. Her hair was spread across his chest in dripping swirls.

"Are you okay, Ryan?" she asked, her voice muffled against him, her breath warm on his skin.

"For the moment." He savored the feel of her clutched to him, knowing she wasn't going to back away. He sincerely hoped Phoebe took a long time getting that towel. "Pardon me if I ask, but under the circumstances, I believe I deserve an explanation."

"What?"

He grinned back at the wide eyes blinking at him. "Are you trying to do me in? First the kick in the face—"

"Chin."

"And then the canoe—"

"You started that one."

"And now, hmm . . . attempted drowning? Is this your way of eliminating the opposition?"

"You're forgetting something, Ryan."

Her face was close to his, and her eyes were gently amused, a look he knew by now was rare. "I don't think so."

"You started this whole thing."

Then she was giggling. He didn't understand the joke, but the effect was pure heaven. She could have accused him of anything and he would have agreed. He was entranced, just like Swamp Monster after pizza.

"You attacked me first, you know."

"I didn't—"

"Yes, you did, when you slid into me in the hall that very first day, remember?"

He nodded slowly, watching the twinkle in her eyes.

"I thought you were crazy."

"Yes, I know."

The flush on her face was not from sunburn. She giggled again, and the sound made him think of tiny silver bells.

"Ryan, believe me, I'm sorry I fell on you," she said. "Phoebe and I were just cooling off and—"

"And I ought to watch where I'm going," he offered, not even trying to sound sorry. He lifted the green spaghetti strap that snaked across his shoulder. "Yes, this is a real nice bathing suit," he said. A chuckle bubbled up and escaped him, and in a few seconds they were both shaking with laughter.

She lifted her head, her clear eyes watering. "I hope your foot isn't broken," she said, gulping back a hiccup.

He shook his head. "Worth it," he gasped.

When Phoebe returned, she eyed the two of them skeptically. "Impressive, Summer," she said, grinning at their efforts to sober. She tossed Summer the towel she'd slung over her shoulders.

"What?" asked Summer, hastily wrapping it around herself.

"I like the way you handle a situation—you know—take charge."

Summer shook her head. "Sometimes you just do it. Especially when a little green bathing suit forces you to." The two women exchanged knowing glances.

Ryan sat up slowly.

"Can you walk at all?" asked Summer.

He tested the swelling ankle and felt pain slice up his leg. Groaning, he eased back down.

"I'll get Joel and the guys," said Phoebe. "They can carry you to the bus." She waded into the surf, shouting.

Summer sat on the sand beside him, this time not quite so close. The sky was now covered with heavy rain-filled clouds, blocking the warmth of the sun. He wanted to feel her body next to his again, and not here on the beach. He wanted her alone, stretched out beside him, her heated flesh melting into his.

"Does it hurt much?" she asked as she tenderly felt his purpling foot.

He shook his head, no. She smelled of salt and sea, a clean sun-baked scent. "I like you this way," he whispered.

"What way?"

"Disheveled." He brushed a speck of sand from her knee.

"Apparently," she said, adjusting the towel, "I end up a mess whenever you're around."

"Somebody's got to do it. Left alone, you'd spend your life prim and proper, sitting in front of a computer."

She tilted her head to study him. "And you don't think that's where I should be."

"Not every waking moment," he said, noticing the sun had turned her nose and cheeks a deep peach color, different from the way she looked when she blushed.

"Carrie didn't really have a garden club meeting today, did she?"

He ran his finger lightly down her cheek. "You've gotten yourself burned," he said, wishing his lips could follow his finger's path.

She touched her skin where his hand had been.

"You did enjoy your day at the beach, didn't you?" he asked.

"Ryan, you could have just come straight out and asked me to go with you."

"You would have said no."

"You're right." Her long lashes fluttered, and she looked away. "You tricked me."

He felt the now-familiar twinge of guilt. For a moment, he wondered if she'd guessed his whole plan. But no, if she did know, she'd pull him back under the waves right now and keep him there. He'd brought her to the beach to keep her away from the clinic, there was no denying that. Every slip of her schedule was making it that much easier for him. But he'd had other reasons too.

His reaction to the pressure of her warm body against his told him much too clearly his motives weren't completely altruistic. And they were becoming less and less so as his body acknowledged her nearness. His eyes couldn't help but follow the long stretch of her legs, his lungs couldn't help but breathe in her delicious scent.

He cleared his throat. "I thought you might be interested in learning something about my clients," he said, resting his hand on her thigh.

"You mean the kids whose lives will be ruined by Humantec?" She pulled the towel more tightly around herself, and he felt her muscles tense under his touch. When she sat up straighter and squared her shoulders, he dropped his hand.

"Looks like you made a friend of Phoebe," he said, knowing he'd better keep his urges to himself for now.

"She misses her mother." Her voice was unexpectedly soft. "I don't think there's ever a way to make up for that."

He could hear the deep sadness in her words, and it pulled at his heart. Summer's protective armor had slipped just enough for him to see what it hid. He wanted to pull her into his arms and hold her tight. She needed it as much as he did.

"Phoebe and her father are learning to support each other," he said instead. "Jimmy's heavy-handed sometimes, but he's trying. He loves her."

Summer sighed, digging her toes into the sand. "Yes, I know. But love isn't always enough."

"You're right," said Ryan. "But it's the best place to start." He took her hand, disquieted at the vulnerability he saw. She pulled away, but the soft feel of her skin lingered on his fingertips. Staring out at the pounding surf, he felt an uneasiness curl itself into his chest, purring low and insistent, like a cat unwilling to be ignored.

She was silent for a moment, staring into the breakers. He watched the color slowly drain from her face. When she turned back to him, her eyes were as dark as the sky. "I don't know what got into me today," she said simply. "I don't usually get involved in other people's lives."

"Summer, I'm glad you did get involved today. You're just what Phoebe needs." And what he needed too. Catching a wisp of hair the wind was blowing across her face, he tucked it carefully behind her ear.

She stiffened her back, but the corners of her mouth curved into a tiny smile.

Summer knew Ryan was in pain, he had to be with a foot swollen three times its size. But on the way back to Sandy Flats, he'd talked and laughed and led the kids through every Beatles song she'd ever heard. When he'd started on a medley of Madonna tunes, she knew he was delirious. She wasn't surprised that he'd quieted down considerably the last twenty miles.

He sat right behind her as she drove the bus back, and she was acutely aware of his every move. She'd even heard his breath catch when he shifted positions, and he'd been very still since they'd entered the town limits.

When they arrived at the hospital, Ryan stumbled getting out of the bus, his weight falling heavily against her. The only thing that kept him from crushing her was Joel's grip on his belt from behind.

"You can let go now, Joel," said Ryan, leaning

against the side of the bus. "Can you get the kids home, Summer?"

"Sure. I can do that. Anything else?"

"Yes." He leaned toward her. "I think I'm slipping."

Summer steadied him, her arms locked around his waist, feeling his warm breath, soft against her neck.

"Thanks," he whispered.

She tried to ignore the pounding of her heart. "Don't mention it," she said, and then bit her lip. Holding him up seemed like the most important task in the world to her at that moment.

An emergency room attendant wheeled out a chair, and he grunted only once, when she and the attendant began to lower him into the chair. As the weight of his body shifted away, she felt an odd sense of separation. It was as if the simple task of holding on to him had consumed her.

She shook off the sinking feeling and looked up at the hospital entrance. It was only a glance but she'd registered the red glare of the word emergency shining out of a harsh white background and the doors gaping like jaws below it as people scurried in and out.

An unreasonable panic rose to her throat. It was a familiar but disconcerting response, dredged from the time she was twelve and her mother lay behind similar doors, suffering through the last weeks of her life.

Summer hugged herself, steadying the tremble that had started in her gut and threatened to rattle down her limbs to her fingertips. She planted her feet firmly on the pavement, willing them not to pull her humiliatingly back into the bus. One more minute, she thought, you can stand here one more minute.

"You coming back for me?" asked Ryan. The touch of his hand on her wrist made her jump, and he looked at her quizzically.

"I . . . the . . . ah, kids. I'll take them all home and—"

"By the time you get back, I'll have been thoroughly processed and packaged and then you can take me home." His words were light, but his face looked ashen under his tan.

"I'll send Marcus back to get you," she said, feeling like a captain deserting his ship. But there was no way she could come back here, not and get through the doors of that hospital.

"Marcus will be able to help you better than I could. And I have to do some work tonight," she said, hastily backing toward the bus before he could argue. He frowned but said nothing, seeming to know she couldn't have handled a plea from him just then.

Summer stood silently as the attendant whisked him up the ramp. Then, she climbed quickly into the bus, not looking back.

Ryan hobbled toward the kitchen. For once he was glad his cottage was small. Just getting through normal housecleaning was taking him all day. His ankle hadn't been broken, but it was plenty sore. He was thankful Summer had been willing to drive the bus back. She'd been a good sport about it all, at least up until they'd arrived at the hospital. He'd learned enough about that straight back to tell him there was something upsetting her, and he suspected it was more than his injury. She seemed to be able to handle just about anything, as long as it didn't require opening her heart.

Still, she'd done remarkably well, taking over for him like she was actually enjoying it. That was a change. He'd always been in the role of caretaker before. When he'd decided to go into counseling, it had been partly because he enjoyed taking care of people. He'd had an image of himself as the champion of the weak and vulnerable.

For a long time he'd fooled himself into thinking he played the part fairly well. But his guardianship failed its harshest test, and his own sister had paid for his error. He knew now he wasn't anyone's champion. He let out a disgusted sigh. It was a self-serving illusion anyway.

He thought of Summer. She didn't need a champion. No, she needed something entirely different.

Propping himself against the counter, he began stacking dishes. He scraped the remains of last night's sandwich into Swamp Monster's bowl, watching the dog scramble delightedly out from beneath a chair. "No question about what you need, is there, boy?" Monster wagged his tail as he wolfed the treat.

He scratched Monster's head absently. Why did he have such a strong urge to go searching for that hidden heart of Summer's? He was certain it would be a mistake to tamper with her defenses, a mistake to even think about it.

He should stop thinking, especially about Summer. It made him hot just imagining the feel of her body pressed hard against him. Oh yes, he'd been cooped up here a couple of days too long. It was definitely time to stop thinking.

He pushed away from the counter and opened the refrigerator door. Its contents were disappointing. He reached for the last beer and downed it in a few hefty swigs. Maybe in a few days he'd be able to handle the Jeep's clutch. He'd have to get out soon, otherwise he'd go crazy, or starve to death. He started the awkward trek back to the sofa.

Swamp Monster gave a small yelp and rushed to the door, tail wagging. Whoever had come visiting, Monster heartily approved. "C'mon in," he called, maneuvering around the old magazine-covered trunk that served as a coffee table. Half-falling, he managed to make it onto the couch. When he looked up, it was Summer standing in the doorway, the evening light playing around her face, touching it with pastel softness.

She wore a narrow, dark skirt that emphasized her slender lines, and a silky pearl-buttoned blouse. He all but forgot his newly made resolution.

How could he not think about Summer? How could he not think about opening one of those buttons after another, slowly, all the way down. Not think about how creamy soft her—

"Hi," she said, holding the grocery bag up. "I thought you might need these." She hesitated. "May I come in?"

He smiled, ridiculously glad she'd come. "Depends on what's in that," he said, pointing to the bag as he eased his foot onto the trunk.

"Just a few snacks," she said, emptying the contents of the bag onto the kitchen counter.

He noticed she'd bought a box of dog biscuits.

Monster noticed, too, but was not being as cool about this unexpected pleasure as he was.

"Since I'm the one who sat on your ankle, by accident I assure you"—her eyes twinkled, daring him to disagree—"I thought I should at least help you out a little." She pulled out a steak. "I didn't know what you liked, so I—"

"Ah, guilt. A powerful emotion." He grinned. "And occasionally worthwhile too."

"I also wanted to apologize for sending Marcus back to the hospital for you," she said, not looking directly at him this time.

His gaze roamed to her shapely legs. "No problem. Marcus took care of everything. He said you went back to the clinic—"

"Yes, well, I did have some programming to work on, but . . ." She rounded the counter and sat down on the trunk, brushing his bandage with her fingertips. "I have a little problem with hospitals. They make me . . . uncomfortable." She smiled weakly. "I don't think hospitals are designed to be hospitable. Do you?" She sounded a little breathless. "They should change the name altogether. It's inaccurate—"

"It's all right." He took her hand. "I'm a big boy. I can handle a hospital. The ankle's just sprained."

Their eyes locked. "I'm sorry," she whispered.

"I don't want to hear you say that again," he said, fiercely ignoring those pearl buttons. "Besides, you were terrific, driving all the way back from the beach, singing those ridiculous songs at the top of your lungs."

"You were the one singing."

"I heard you, too, don't deny it." He focused on her lower lip. "Thanks for taking over for me, Summer. I hadn't originally planned on making you work quite so hard."

"I'm just sor—"

"Summer."

"It slipped out," she said softly. Then she wet her lips and seemed to hold her breath for a moment, as if deliberating over something.

"What is it?" he asked, studying the soft lines of her face. Was it anything like the urges bombarding him at this moment?

"It was a good idea, you know."

"What?"

"Inviting, no, coercing me to the beach. I'm glad I went. I haven't had that much fun since—" She shook her head. "Since our canoe trip. And before that, I don't even remember . . ."

He touched her cheek. "So I'm forgiven for my little trick?"

"Well, yes. But I don't like being manipulated."

"I'm sorry," he said.

"If I can't say that, neither can you."

He sighed. Whether he could say it or not, he had a feeling he was going to be a lot sorrier if things kept going the way they were. He should stop what he was doing right now, but he didn't.

He pulled her gently to him, kissing her lightly. Did she feel the same tingling electric charge that was fueling his exploration? All of her outward signals remained cool, controlled, but he sensed something quiet different just below the surface. It was like reading a very subtle language—a language that intrigued him like nothing else could.

He had no legitimate claim to what she held inside.

Perhaps it was a habit of his profession to knock on a door until it opened. But no, this was more. He wasn't just knocking on any door. If he wasn't careful, he'd rattle this one right off its hinges. All he was certain of was that at this moment, he was quickly becoming a driven man. He gathered her into his arms, ignoring her thin crust of resistance, tuning instead to the lambent flame he knew was beneath it.

He savored the perfect softness of her lips more deeply and felt the heat of his own desire rise with unexpected force. He slid his hands down her exquisite back, moving her against him. When she responded with a tiny gasp, he took a long breath and fought desperately for control. He didn't want to scare her back into her shell, not now.

"Summer," he whispered, nestling her in his arms, feeling her yield as she leaned into him. There was more to this woman than her exterior of calm rationality, so much more.

Trembling, she ran her fingers through his hair and smiled at him. He nuzzled her ear, tenderly, teasingly. Oh, how he needed to touch her, to experience every inch of her. Only the faint ringing of the phone kept him from loosing himself in her warm compliance.

"Don't get up—I'll answer it," she said in a small, breathless voice, quickly unwinding herself from his embrace. "Hello?"

He watched her shapely brows knit in concern. "Who is it?" he whispered, struggling up from the couch.

"Jimmy Prescot," she mouthed back.

"I'll take it."

She held up a finger, signaling him to wait. "Can I

talk with Phoebe?" he heard her ask as he hobbled toward the phone.

She pressed the receiver against her chest. "I think he's done something to Phoebe. He's awfully upset."

Ryan said a quick, silent prayer and took the phone.

"I've got to talk with you right now," said Jimmy, his voice shaking with emotion.

"Hold on, Jimmy. Just tell me what's happened."

"It's Phoebe. We're at the store. Can you come out —please?"

"Is she all right?"

"I think so." Jimmy was breathing hard. "I can't talk to her," he said, "I . . . I locked her up."

"I'm on my way," said Ryan. He wasn't sure what he'd find, but he knew he'd better get to that store fast.

Summer touched his elbow. "What happened?" she asked.

"I'm not sure. He said she was okay, whatever that means. I'll have to go out there."

Her eyes darkened. "I'll drive you."

"Thanks." He squeezed her hand. "But please, Summer, remember one thing, you're just the chauffeur. I'm trained to handle situations like this, it's my job. We don't know what to expect, and I want you to stay out of it."

"Then you should have thought of that before you introduced us. Phoebe and I are friends now, remember? Maybe I can help."

There was no time to argue with the woman standing before him, hands placed firmly on her hips. "Just remember," he said, "you're not the therapist tonight, I am."

Jimmy Prescot was standing in the parking lot of his store when they pulled in. "I'm afraid I've done it now," he called, hurrying to meet them.

"Settle down, Jimmy. We'll get this straightened out," said Ryan. "Take some deep breaths and relax." He gave Summer a warning look and then turned all his attention to Jimmy Prescot. "Now, tell me what this is all about."

"I had to lock Phoebe in the storeroom," said Jimmy, clenching his fists. "She's in there now. She came into the store with that Speedy, damn him. He started talkin' smart, said my daughter, my own daughter didn't have to answer to me. I told Phoebe she had to git on home. This guy's trouble. Do you understand me? He's too rough for my little girl." His voice shook with anger. "Phoebe started bawling and saying she was gonna run off. I had to lock her up, don't you see? She's my baby . . ." His eyes glistened, and he looked away.

Ryan's calm tone was measured for reassurance. He didn't smell whiskey on Jimmy's breath, good. The man could be rough when he'd been drinking. "Where's the boy she was with?" he asked.

"I ran him off, and he better not come back here or I'll get my gun next time."

He knew full well Jimmy would do anything to protect his daughter. "Let's go inside and see about Phoebe," he said.

Jimmy unlocked the storeroom, and Ryan watched as the look of misery on Phoebe's face hardened into hatred. She turned her back to her father.

"It's time we git on home now, Phoebe," said Jimmy gruffly.

"Go away," she said, not looking at him. "I don't want to go anywhere with you. You might as well lock me back up, 'cause I'm not gonna follow your rules anymore, Daddy, not ever." She choked back a sob. "I'd rather be dead."

"Now hold on here," said Jimmy, his voice rising, "I'm your father, and you'll do as I say. Git yourself outta there right now or I'll—"

"Or you'll what?" asked Phoebe icily.

"I'll—"

"Wait a minute, Jimmy," said Ryan. The two needed time to cool off. If the current exchange continued, it would only make it more difficult for father and daughter to resolve anything. He motioned Jimmy away from the storeroom.

"I'm gonna git her outta there, Doc, if I have to skin her alive . . ."

"Excuse me."

They both looked up to see Summer calmly surveying them from the doorway. "I wonder if I might have a chat with Phoebe, alone."

"C'mon, Jimmy," said Ryan, "let's go sit on the dock. I need to get off this foot, and you need to settle down a bit."

"I wouldn't be all fired up if—"

"I understand. Let's just give the ladies a minute together. It can't hurt," he coaxed, giving Summer a nod.

With an encouraging smile directed toward Jimmy, Summer stepped into the storeroom and closed the door behind her.

Ryan sat on a bench just outside the store, watching Jimmy pace back and forth in front of him.

"I don't understand her," said Jimmy. " 'Til her ma died, she was the sweetest kid you could ever hope to have. Now look at her. Back talkin' and hanging around God only knows what kinda people. I'm gonna get that Speedy feller if it's the—"

"Do you think that will turn Phoebe back into your sweet little girl?"

Jimmy stopped pacing and frowned. "Least she'd stay home," he said slowly.

"Or find someone else."

"Damn." Jimmy's wild eyes began to cloud. "I love her so much," he said quietly.

"I know you do, Jimmy. And you don't want anything to hurt your daughter," he said.

"Damn right."

"So you lock her up."

Jimmy shook his head. "Nuthin' else's workin'."

"You're scared for her, aren't you?"

He nodded. "Yeah—Kid's a lot of responsibility to have alone."

"And you're alone now." Ryan heard him gulp back his emotion. And then Jimmy began to talk. About his wife, how much he missed her, and how close the family had once been.

Ryan listened.

"They'll be okay for tonight," said Ryan as he rolled down the window of the van. The warm air rushed past his face, bearing the clean scent of pine. "Jimmy hadn't been drinking, and I think he got a few things off his chest. But what I want to know is how you calmed Phoebe down."

Summer shrugged, her hands tight on the steering wheel. "I didn't do much, just let her cry on my shoulder." She inhaled deeply and cleared her throat.

"Are you going to be all right?"

She nodded, keeping her eyes on the road. He suspected those were tears she was blinking back. Phoebe had needed someone to cry with, and now he wondered if Summer did too. He squeezed her shoulder, wanting to take her in his arms again. "Look, I know you helped back there. But situations like this can take a lot out of you. If you're not prepared to handle—"

"I can certainly handle this," she said. "I've always been able to control . . ." Her voice cracked, and she fell silent.

"Pull over," he said.

"What?"

"Pull over, here . . . That's right."

"What is it?"

As the van rolled to a stop, he slid across the seat, and put his arm around the soft curve of her shoulders. He wasn't sure what he could say or do to get through to her, but at this moment, he was convinced that whatever the cost, he wanted to clear those shadow-filled eyes.

"Summer," he said gently, "don't deny your feelings. It's okay to let them out." He felt her stiffen in his arms but he would not let go, not now. "There's a big difference between handling emotions and controlling them."

"That sounds like something a psychologist would

say." She kept her eyes forward, trained on the darkness beyond the windshield.

"It's true," he said softly.

"Maybe for some people."

He watched her delicate fingers wrap tightly around the steering wheel. He wanted to touch her, not just physically, but to reach down into that spot he knew was somewhere deep inside her, alone and afraid.

"Ryan, I learned early on how to take care of myself, and one of the first lessons was going on, no matter what's happening inside."

"But—"

"My father taught me." She lowered her chin, and he could no longer see her eyes. "He never faltered an instant."

He could hear her strained breathing.

"When I felt like everything was falling apart, he was right there." Her voice fell to a whisper. "There was no time to stop and cry," she said. "Not over Mom, not over anything. It was hard, but we went on."

"Summer, you're not your father."

"I've lived by his rules a long time. I can't do it any other way."

He put his hand over hers, feeling the tension in her curved fingers. She was gripping the steering wheel as if it were the only thing keeping her afloat. "Summer—"

"It's Phoebe and her dad who need therapy, Ryan, not me," she said, her voice strengthening now. "I'm not one of your clients."

"I want to help, Summer. I care about you, you're upset and—"

She pushed him away and glared at him. "Thank

you. However, I am perfectly fine," she said, precisely enunciating each word.

He relented, shifting back to his side of the seat. "I'm here to listen whenever you're ready to talk," he said, making himself stay away from her. She should be held, he thought, for a long, long time. But he knew she wouldn't let him, not tonight.

The van jerked as she steered it back onto the road. "You should be worrying about Phoebe," she said stiffly. "Not me."

SEVEN

"Phoebe, this is a very bad idea," said Summer, wishing she could get the girl to see Ryan, but her refusal had been adamant. "If you'd just let me call Dr. Jericho."

Phoebe hiked her backpack higher on her shoulder and stepped down from the porch of Alford Place. "He'd just try to talk me out of it. And don't you try. You can't stop me. I thought you'd understand about Speedy. I guess you don't."

"But I do. Phoebe, you just can't—"

"I can't stay another minute with Daddy. He's completely unreasonable."

"Your father loves you, Phoebe. If you'll give him a chance—"

"Please." Phoebe's eyes pleaded with her for support. "I thought I could trust you." She rubbed her fingertips against her temple. "You seemed to know just how I felt. That's why I thought I could count on you to understand."

"Oh, I do." Summer took a deep breath, aware of the faint scent of Carrie's magical garden floating on the morning mists. She could use a little otherworldly help right now.

"When my mother died, my life changed drastically too," she said softly. "Sometimes I think my father's rules and regulations were his comfort—not mine, but I know they were all he had to give. You have to be patient with your dad."

Phoebe stared down the drive.

Speedy would be here any minute and, short of locking her up, Summer could do nothing to stop the girl from going with him. She combed her fingers roughly through her tousled hair and tried to think of what Ryan would do in this situation. But she had none of his special magic; she wasn't reaching the girl.

Phoebe had shown up just after supper, and she'd encouraged her to stay and talk—thinking of Jimmy's hot temper and not wanting Phoebe to end up in the storeroom like she had three days ago. Ryan had warned her about playing therapist.

She picked at the strap on Phoebe's backpack, wondering what she'd do if she had a storeroom handy. Phoebe stepped out into the drive, as if half-expecting to be manhandled into the house. Summer knew then she was losing her.

They had talked all night. She'd thought Phoebe was coming around, that she understood it was possible to learn to get along with her dad. But this morning, Phoebe insisted that she had to leave.

Anger had been Summer's first reaction. Now, it gave way to fear as she heard the unmistakable rumble of a car engine in the distance.

"Well, I guess this is it," said Phoebe, giving her a strained smile. "I can't stay with Daddy, I can't. We'll just keep hurting each other." She put a slender hand on Summer's sleeve. "Please explain it to him, and to Dr. Jericho." She didn't look back when she hurried to the old pickup truck that had screeched to a stop in front of them.

"Phoebe wait . . . Please," she called, but her words were drowned out by the truck's roar.

The loud knock on the door of her room made Summer jump. Her nerves were stretched taut from frantic phone calls, and the day had hardly begun. She flung the door open expectantly. "Any news?"

Ryan stepped in, hesitating briefly as his gaze swept the room before settling on her.

"Well?" she prompted, her spirits sinking as she read the answer in his sagging shoulders. "Oh Ryan, it's all my fault. I tried to stop her, but I couldn't. I didn't know how to convince her to stay. So stupid . . . stupid." Her words tumbled out faster than she could think. "I messed things up. I shouldn't have gotten involved. You were right—"

"Hey, steady there. Maybe no one could've kept her from going. It'll be all right," he said, his voice low and calm. "I promise. Phoebe will get through this, and so will you."

The tenderness in his look laid her heart bare as she struggled against the hot tears stinging her eyes. The coat of determined rationality that had held her together all night was crumbling into a thousand useless pieces. "Oh Ryan, nothing's predictable anymore. I don't know what to do."

He pulled her gently into his warm, solid embrace.

It felt so safe. She buried her face against the rough fabric of his shirt, letting a tiny sob escape. Quickly she realized she shouldn't have allowed herself even that. Another sob came on the heels of the first, and then another and another, releasing an uncontrollable torrent. It frightened her to the core. And still she could only cling to Ryan, letting the tears flow.

How wrong, how terribly wrong, she'd been—about everything. She had thought she knew what she was doing. She thought she could help Phoebe. But that had been a stupid assumption. A mistake, a dangerously naive mistake.

The quiet spot, deep within, where she'd safely stored all her doubt and fear had vanished. It was as if the rock she'd always leaned on had crumbled to dust. Darkness filled its place. Darkness and the sound of her own crying. There were no walls around her for protection, no ceiling, no floor to stand on.

She couldn't stiffen her legs against their insistent buckling. Ryan held on to her, his support her only anchor in the storm of emotion that was descending upon her with such unexpected viciousness. It had been a long, exhausting night.

Tenderly, Ryan lifted and carried her to the bed. She did not protest. She could not. He laid her down and then sat beside her on the bed, smoothing back her hair in gentle strokes. "Let it go," he whispered, "let it all out."

His careful, easy touch reached her where no words could go. *Ryan. Ryan is here with me.* The knowledge wrapped around her, warm and secure. There was no one else who could hold her like this.

After a long time, her tears slowed. She looked up,

and her attention was immediately riveted to the expression of deep concern chiseled into Ryan's face. His eyes were trained on her with such intensity that it pulled her back from that formless, frightening world, back to her senses. The tightness in her chest eased, leaving behind a strange quiver.

"What can I do to make it right?" she asked, grasping at the threads of her composure. "I . . . I have to do something."

"I've notified the authorities," he said, stroking her cheek. "They're watching for Phoebe. And I've talked with everyone she might contact. Now, all we can do is wait."

Summer smiled tentatively.

"That's better." He bent over her and kissed her lightly on the forehead.

His hair tickled as it brushed across her face. He smelled good—of soap and comfort. Her body reacted, moving close, her arms entwining his neck and pulling him down to her. She returned his kiss full on the mouth, sending ripples of charged awareness through every nerve. She blinked, startled at the urges rising within her.

"Summer," said Ryan.

"Yes?"

"You took a chance, reaching out to Phoebe." The strength of his gaze held her steady. "I'm glad you did that. Too often we don't know when to reach out, we don't take that chance. You did."

"But it turned out horribly—"

"Whatever happens, Summer, you did the right thing." He put his hands on her shoulders. "It wasn't wrong for you to reach out to Phoebe. Do you understand?" He squeezed, as if he didn't already have her full attention.

"Yes," she said, feeling an unstoppable pull from the dark indigo eyes that had captured her.

"You were willing to accept Phoebe. To let her in. She needed that. We all need that." He leaned forward, pinning her gently against the pillows, a hand resting on either side of her head. "Even you, Summer." He lowered toward her, touching his nose to hers, his lips moving feather-light to caress her cheek and down her jawline.

She lay very still. The heat deep inside her growing, surging at each new touch until it coursed steadily through her trembling body. Ryan's mouth angled over her expectant lips in a slow caress. She strained toward him, meeting his sensuous exploration with her own.

He lifted away, and she felt only the need to pull him back, to cover her sudden chill with his warmth. He cupped her chin and ran his thumb slowly along her lower lip. "Summer," he said huskily. "What hurt has kept you away from this, away from life?"

His words burned toward her heart. He couldn't know how she felt—the fear that was always so near, that had to be hidden. Her father had thought she was so obedient. Max was convinced it was hopeless devotion to work. It was neither.

This was her burden, a private, soul-deep burden that she could not share. All she was sure of was that caring about someone hurt. There were no exceptions. It was as simple and tragic as that.

"Summer, I can see it in your eyes," said Ryan. "You're going somewhere else, somewhere dark and lonely. It doesn't have to be that way." He hadn't moved, but she could sense every inch of his body stretching out along the length of hers. "Let me hold you," he said. "That's all, just hold you." He drew her to him, cuddling her in the safe cocoon of his arms.

"I don't understand what's happening to me," she whispered when she could trust her voice. "I think I'm going crazy."

"No. You're not crazy at all. Just stop thinking." He cradled her head, kissing her gently until she felt heated to the bone. Submerged in the delicate tinglings awakened by his caresses, she abandoned the struggle to force order into her ragged thoughts. She arched against him as his hands moved down her back, her mind fogging in the sudden fire that raced along her spine.

"No walls between us," he murmured, his kiss deepening into a question her body answered blindly. The feel of his hands playing tenderly over her, of his lips possessing hers, was a healing balm, making her whole with endless, nurturing heat. His touch roamed beneath her thin blouse, burning against her sensitized skin, tantalizing her body into mindless molding, hot flesh touching hotter until she no longer knew where her skin ended and his began.

She felt the waistband of her skirt give. At Ryan's gentle touch the growing fire within her licked the soft region below. An ache began in her lower abdomen, an ache that begged to be satisfied as the slow movement of his fingers between her thighs turned into exquisite torture.

And she wanted more. She wanted all of him.

The realization brought the stampede of her senses to a crushing halt. She stiffened, every inch of her body paralyzed, suspended in a sudden throb while her mind fought to clear.

"Summer?" Ryan's voice was husky.

She lay in his arms, unable to move, wanting to remember this moment. She looked at the canopy above her, memorizing its cream ruffles, at the armoire and its dark ornate carving, and finally at Ryan's rugged features. If she could love, it would be this man. But she could not. And he deserved more, so much more—a love that would pierce the darkness in his eyes. A love that wasn't afraid to grow and bloom in the glare of the sun. She couldn't give him that.

Ryan stirred beside her. "I'm not going to hurt you, Summer," he said.

She traced the line of his jaw with her finger and felt the muscles tighten under his tanned skin. "I know." Her throat constricted, and she breathed deeply to keep her mind clear. "I don't think this is . . . wise."

He pulled away slowly. "Does it need to be?"

"Ryan, I'm sorry. I—"

"No. Don't be. I care about you, Summer. You deserve to feel good." His pulse throbbed in a vein along his neck.

Summer's struggle to fight against his comforting warmth made her head ache as she clumsily adjusted her blouse and smoothed her skirt.

He sat up, running his hand over his face as if just waking, and stared at the floor. He shook his head. "Summer, I'm not going to push you. I never want to do that," he said. "I'll go now."

"No. Don't." She'd uttered the words before thinking. But she didn't want him to leave. Not yet. She couldn't bear being alone right now. "Please stay. Talk to me. Just talk to me." She couldn't believe what she was doing, but she couldn't help herself.

He looked at her, one eyebrow raised. A small smile curled his lips. "If you insist." He stood slowly and pulled a chair to the side of the bed. "But I'd better move over here. It might be . . . ah . . . easier." He sat down, stretching his long legs out in front of him, and leaned back, hands clasped behind his back. "So. What do you want to talk about?"

"Anything," she said, anything to keep her heart from rattling around in the emptiness. "This room," she said, grabbing at the first thought that occurred to her. "Is there something about it you don't like?"

He was slow to answer. "Why do you ask?" he said, his gaze settling on the heavy armoire. "Has Aunt Carrie been talking to you?"

"No," said Summer, her interest piqued. It wasn't her imagination after all.

"This was Alicia's room," he said, not taking his eyes off the carving above the door of the armoire.

There was a tension in his voice Summer had never heard before. She weighed her curiosity against her fear of learning too much about this man, but couldn't stop herself from asking. "Is this where she—?"

"Died? Yes. On the floor beside this bed," he said softly.

"Oh."

"I know it must sound strange to someone as rational as you are, Summer, but there was a time when I could feel her very strongly in here—her sadness, her confusion."

Summer started to reach for him but she quelled

the urge before her hand could move from her lap. She couldn't help him.

He closed his eyes, whether to shut out the memory —or to brand it in more deeply, she could not tell. "I usually end up here whenever I come to Alford Place. It started just after Alicia's death. I'd make my pilgrimage all the way to the door." He sighed. "But I could never quite make myself go in." He opened his eyes and smiled, his liquid gaze meeting hers. She felt her heart catch.

"I imagined the ritual would help me cope. You know us psychologists are always trying to find better ways to do that." He laughed but there was no humor in his eyes.

Oh, how she wanted to pull him to her, to hold on tightly until she'd soothed his pain away. But it would not be enough. Death couldn't be cuddled away.

"I'm sorry," she said before she'd even thought. Such small words, weak words that seemed to die even as they left her lips. But they were all she could manage, all she dared. Now she understood why he didn't want her to say them.

"I've battled that doorjamb for months," said Ryan, folding his arms across his chest. "It wasn't until you showed up that I crossed it. Sounds odd, but I ought to thank you."

"I don't understand."

He looked at her, the warmth coming back to his eyes. "You don't need to." He leaned forward. "You make it better, Summer. That's all I know."

"The first night I was here, I liked this room," she said, swallowing the sudden dryness in her throat. "I even pretended this bed was a cream puff."

He looked at her skeptically.

"It's true. And I snuggled down inside of it."

He shook his head. "I can't quite picture Summer Keeton, Humantec wiz kid, inside a cream puff, make-believe or not."

"Well I was," she said. "And I felt welcomed, in a strange way."

"Summer," Ryan said, leaning over and pulling at a lock of her hair, twisting it around his fingers. "I meant that thank you."

"But I didn't do anything."

"Yes, you did. You are doing something now."

He cupped her chin and kissed her, his lips warm and lingering. She stifled a groan and made herself turn away. "I . . . I think it's time for you to go now."

The printer hummed into action, and Summer leaned back in her chair, watching the program code streak in uneven black lines across the paper. She'd immersed herself in programming the moment she entered the clinic that morning. It had been the same every day since Phoebe disappeared.

But she'd quit trying to work during the evenings. When the clinic emptied at five each day, it wasn't long after that Summer left too. She wanted to be available if Phoebe came back, not locked in some dark building. Carrie had promised to call if Phoebe showed up at Alford Place, but her reassurance wasn't enough.

Summer looked at her watch, torn between programming and returning to Alford Place. It was almost seven. She'd finish printing this program and take it with her. At least she could go over the changes later that night. She still had a job to do, whether she was working at peak efficiency or not. There was a lot of work to finish in the next two and a half weeks. She hadn't even trained everyone on the office automation software, much less the data base accesses.

"Taking a break, I see. Now that's a change." Ryan stood outside her office door, holding a small white bag in one hand and a spoon in the other. "You like ice cream, don't you?"

She smiled, her mood lightening. "I love it."

He moved a stack of printouts and sat down on her desk. "Close your eyes and open your mouth."

She obeyed instantly and was rewarded with a cold, sweet taste on her tongue. "Chocolate?"

"Mocha mint."

"Yum."

"Hold still," said Ryan, kissing away the smudge he'd managed to get on her nose. His sticky lips tickled, and she felt a quiver of excitement at the bottom of her stomach.

The phone's intruding buzz halted her in midgiggle. "It might be Carrie," she said quickly, reaching around him to grab the receiver.

"Hello? Oh . . . Max."

She looked at Ryan and shrugged. He put the ice-cream carton down and slid off the desk. "Don't leave," she whispered, wondering at the sudden stiffening of his broad shoulders.

"No, Max, I am not aware of any problems. The project is going as smooth as . . . as mocha mint." She held the receiver away from her face and helped herself to another spoonful, motioning to Ryan to sit

back down. He shook his head and walked to the door,
his face a darkening mask.

Max interrupted. "Summer . . . Summer, are you
still there?"

"Yes." The ice cream melted pleasantly around her
tongue.

"I received a call from Roscoe today. Were you
aware that Sandy Flats is hedging on the system?"

"They're what?"

"I said, they're ready to back out. How's the data
base module look? It's done, isn't it? If it is, we've got
'em."

The line crackled, and she wondered if she'd heard
him correctly. "What do you mean? They've already
bought the entire package. That's the usual agreement."

"I had to negotiate differently this time. We needed
financing to get into the overseas deal, that, by the way,
has gone over big—"

"Stop right there." She dropped the spoon into the
carton and turned her back to Ryan. "Since when have
you started changing the way we do these contracts?"
she whispered. "We are partners, remember?"

"I know. But Roscoe was under a lot of pressure. I
told you I had to do a little dancing around there."

"So, just what kind of dancing are we talking about
here?" she asked, her stomach tightening.

"Don't worry. Sandy Flats clinic committed to
phase one, hardware, networking software, and basic
office automation. The data base module just needed to
be in within the month. If it is, they can't back out."

"What?"

"Summer, don't get wound up."

"I'm not. I just—"

"Listen. You always do a magnificent job. You've got a special talent here. Working sixteen hours a day gets things done. I knew we couldn't lose. You can make a june bug fly into a duck's mouth in no time flat. Why, you can—"

"Max—"

"Knowing your schedule, I'll bet you've already trained on those data bases."

"But, Max—"

"I'm sure there's nothing to worry about. Right? Summer, it's just that I promised the system would be up and running within a month instead of the usual six weeks. That's your normal schedule anyway, no problem."

"And if the data base is not up?" Summer held her breath.

"The clinic isn't obligated to go with the entire package."

"Oh."

"Just remember, I'm counting on you. Do this one for us. Then the Bombay deal will put Humantec over the top. We'll be in the big time like we planned. Summer, we're so close, I can taste it."

Summer stared at Ryan's back, a chill creeping over her as she tried to read the small movement between his shoulder blades.

"How do we stand anyway?" said Max.

"I'm sitting."

"Summer?"

"Oh, we're . . . fine."

She picked up the spoon and stabbed it into the mocha mint, her stomach folding in on itself.

"Max," she said, stirring the melting ice cream slowly. "I'll give you a report at the end of the week. I'll know where we stand by then." She was afraid to say more.

"That's just what I want to hear. You're doing a terrific job."

"Yes, great," she said unenthusiastically.

"I wasn't kidding about Bombay."

"I know." She replaced the phone in its cradle and straightened the cord in carefully precise movements, then she took a deep breath. "Ryan."

He turned to her, his face was rigid, but she saw what she'd dreaded in his eyes. "That was—"

"Maxwell Pelion," he said. His voice had a distinct edge to it.

"Ryan, did you know about the contract arrangement?" she asked, hoping the suspicions that were creeping insidiously into her mind were unfounded.

"I told you I was fighting Humantec," he said flatly.

"I'm way off schedule, you know."

"I'm aware of that."

"And you know why I'm off schedule too." She swallowed the lump forming in her throat. "Don't you, Ryan?"

"I know that I've tried to get you to take some time to find out what we do here and—"

"You deliberately kept me from finishing those data bases," she said, wishing he'd deny it, hoping he'd convince her otherwise.

"Yes, I did."

His words froze in a cold, hard lump in the pit of her stomach.

"My plan wasn't intended to hurt you."

"Your plan? I see." The lump in her stomach grew, chilling her entire body.

"No, you don't see." He took a step toward her. "I was trying to—"

"Stop." The tears that might have come hardened icily behind her dry eyes. "Max's special contract was quite the loophole, wasn't it?" She thought her voice sounded amazingly controlled. "You just had to keep me from doing my job—"

"We've gone beyond that, Summer." He took another step but she backed away, certain that a touch from him would shatter the glacier she'd become.

"Please, believe me," he said. She tried to close her ears to the rich baritone that had lulled her into this disaster. "I admit, I meant to keep Humantec from finishing the project on time. I told you I had to fight it."

"Yes, you did. And if I had kept my mind on my job, I wouldn't have the problem, you would."

"Summer—" He reached out, his deep blue eyes shining, imploring her to come to him.

She gritted her teeth. "You've won this skirmish, but I don't concede defeat, not yet."

"I told you once before, Summer, this isn't a war," he said, with a tone of exasperation. "Don't you understand yet?"

Anger plunged claws into her heart, digging up the tiny seed of trust that had dared to germinate there. "You know something, Ryan? You are a master manipulator," she said with venom. "Yes, one of the best. You're much better than I could ever hope to be." She paced the floor, unable to look at him, unable to watch the wounds she was inflicting. "I've never insinuated myself into someone's personal life, into someone's heart to win a contract for Humantec. That's under-handed, Dr. Jericho, and dirty."

"You've got it all wrong. I didn't—"

"You did, you can't deny it. Can you?" She didn't wait for his answer. "Please, go." She stood at the door to usher him out.

The look he turned on her was defiant. "I'm not leaving until you understand," he said, closing the door. "You're going to hear this, Summer, whether you want to or not."

She steeled her mind against him, needing to think, something she'd done much too little of lately. All she could feel was icy betrayal. The more he explained, the colder it became.

He stood in front of the door, blocking her exit. "Summer, whatever you think of me, please know that things have changed," he said. "I need you to believe that all that's happened between us is—"

"A lie. Now, let me leave, Ryan." She started around him, but he took her wrist, squeezing it tight in his strong grasp.

"You're shutting me out because of a phone call, Summer Keeton. I'm the same man who held you in his arms and—"

"No!" She wrenched free.

His eyebrows raised.

"You definitely aren't what you pretend to be," she said. The lines of his face hardened frighteningly. "I don't know who you are. All I know is you've used me." His eyes held hers, and beneath the anger, she saw pain.

"And you, Humantec wonder girl—I don't suppose

you've ever used anyone," he said, his voice low but lethal.

She braced herself. Go on, say it, she thought. Words she could fight, words would make her strong against him. He looked down at the red mark he'd made on her wrist and ran his fingers across it. The gentleness of his caress stabbed at her heart with more power than the most bitter invective.

She pulled her hand away. "There was never anything between us, Ryan. And it's not over for Humantec. I'm not giving up on the Sandy Flats installation. Not yet."

"I'm not giving up either," he said, his voice gravelly. He opened the door and stepped out.

In a daze, Summer sat down at her computer, listening to the sound of his footsteps receding down the hall. She scrolled the paper out of the printer, moving like a robot, her actions stiff and mechanical. She scanned program code, unable to read the words blurring in front of her.

She was just an obstacle to his cause—one he found a way around. All he had to do was seduce her from the project. If the deadlines weren't met, no contract. How could she be so stupid? She knew better than that. She knew better than to trust her heart to someone.

As she stared at her printout, a gray determination coated the hurt, sealing it deep inside her, encapsulating it like a drum of chemical waste. She would never let her heart corrode again. Humantec was her priority. It had to be that way, she understood now.

It was tough to set up a demonstration for the board of trustees on such short notice, but it had been necessary to work fast. If she was going to salvage this project, she knew she would have to put on a showstopper and she was going to do just that.

She flipped her notebook from palm to palm as she watched the clock. In a few minutes they would call her in for the presentation and it would be up to her to repair the damage she'd done.

Jumbled voices from the conference room seeped through the closed door. Strain as she might, she could not quite make out words. For an instant she thought she heard Ryan's distinctive baritone. But no, her mind was playing tricks. Thankfully, only Roscoe Williams and the board members were to be present. Ryan was not on her list of people to woo. She tried to ignore the vague aching that swept through her at the thought of him.

How could she keep Ryan out of her mind when just a streak of sunlight on water or the scent of gardenia would conjure up his image? The cold, hard lump in her chest reminded her to keep trying.

She rummaged through her purse and found her compact. Think of the presentation—nothing else, she told herself as she checked her makeup. She patted in a wisp of hair that had escaped her sleek style. Good, she looked normal enough. The familiar cool, collected Summer stared back at her, showing no damage. She put the compact away and smoothed her gray suit, adjusted the collar of her black crepe blouse, unbuttoning the top two buttons. She would use all of her assets today, and her battle uniform was one of them—well cut—just right to pique interest but maintain a strictly professional look. She'd chosen the outfit with the same precise care she'd used to design this special demonstration.

She breathed deeply, focusing her mind on her presentation, walking through it step by detailed step to keep any other thoughts from disrupting her concentration. Too soon, the squeak of an opening door wrenched her from her mental safe house.

"Good afternoon, Ms. Keeton," said Roscoe, his voice stiffly formal. "I believe we're ready for you now."

She scanned the faces in the room as she was being introduced. All seemed mildly interested, good enough for a start.

"And, I believe you already know Dr. Jericho," said Roscoe, motioning behind her.

Summer's throat went dry.

"Good morning." The low, smooth voice that greeted her was unmistakably Ryan's.

She turned slowly, keeping her features composed against the hideous pounding of her heart.

"I believe you promised me a demo a while back," he said, casually taking a seat. He looked as formidable an adversary as she'd ever encountered. His black suit and massive build dominated the room. All eyes had strayed from her to the large man who was sitting down next to her.

The smile on her face was sheer force of will. She counted to ten twice before trusting her voice, wishing he had at least chosen a chair farther away. His close proximity could sabotage her mind like sugar in a gas tank. *It won't,* she insisted. *Calm down. You can pull this off. Don't think of anything but the project.*

Summer launched her presentation with an energy borne of teeth-gritting determination. Relying on all the skills she had, she set about projecting confidence into every word, every movement. Except for one man, she watched her audience carefully. Whenever she detected doubts, she reassured. Whenever she noted interest, she elaborated, describing Humantec's system in words that glowed with promise.

When she was ready to concentrate on the details of her data base, she directed the group's attention to a large screen. She had linked it to her computer at the back of the room where she moved to take her place at the keyboard.

Ryan followed.

"Need to stretch this bum leg," he said, shrugging at his infirmity.

Summer's fingers, poised gracefully over the keys, stiffened like granite as he leaned against the wall behind her.

"Please, go on. I can look over your shoulder just fine," he said, his smooth voice snagging on her ragged nerves.

As she brought up the first menu screen, Ryan leaned forward, looking more closely. She focused on the screen in front of her and plowed on, ignoring him with self-defeating intensity.

Once, when she was pointing out the efficient, mouse-driven design, her elbow grazed his midsection. Feeling her face heat, she lost her train of thought. She'd recovered the next instant, but he had seen her hesitation. From then on, it seemed he intentionally stood maddeningly close.

His "accidental" touches sent distracting tingles

racing through her. Angered and frightened at her body's callous betrayal, she fought to keep her attention locked on her computer.

"I think you'll see that without these data bases, the system isn't nearly as powerful as you need," she concluded, using her most professional, agree-with-me smile.

"Oh, yes." It was Roscoe Williams who spoke first. "I certainly think the data bases are—"

"Of course they make it better," said Ryan, "but what are we having to give up to get this?" he said, pointing to the multicolored screen glowing in front of Summer. "Tell me." He walked slowly to the front of the room, his just noticeable limp adding to the impact of his words. "Can this admittedly fine technology take the place of direct service to our clients?" He thumped the big screen as if it were an overripe melon. "Our budget cannot fully support both. We must make a choice, Humantec . . . or humanity."

"Ah . . . if I might add something here—" said Summer.

He glared a clearly readable "No," but said nothing.

She squared her shoulders and stood, waiting for attention to pivot to her end of the room. "Our other installations have documented significant gains in efficiency and effectiveness." She made eye contact with each of the directors and William Roscoe as she spoke, avoiding the one laser blue gaze she knew was trained on her. "The information made available with our system helps to offset the cost. Over a period of a very few years—"

"Our clients don't have years to wait." Ryan's tone

was unyielding. "It's not just a matter of the system shown here." He gestured at the screen, his voice lowering to a compelling urgency. "Decisions to channel resources away from direct client support pull this clinic away from its purpose. Sandy Flats must be here for the people first."

Summer was just forming a rebuttal to deflate the impact of his words when Roscoe stood. "You have raised legitimate concerns here, Dr. Jericho," he said. "Funding for your halfway house has received a number of setbacks. There's no doubt that further erosion of client-directed resources will have a serious impact."

Summer was silent, knowing that Roscoe was picking up on what she had already sensed. She couldn't assure the board that they wouldn't lose client services to technology. How could she know how Sandy Flats was funding her system? It wasn't supposed to be her problem. But somehow, over the past few weeks, it had become hers.

She thought of Phoebe and realized she had stopped short of what Max would have expected her to do.

Going for the sale at all costs was Max Pelion's prime objective. It had to be, otherwise Humantec would have floundered in that first year. But she hadn't been able to bring herself to minimize the impact Humantec was having on Sandy Flats services. She presented her system the best way she could in good conscience. But was it enough?

EIGHT

Summer's face showed faint lines of fatigue, ones Ryan hadn't seen since she'd first arrived in Sandy Flats. He didn't think she'd slept much, was most likely skipping meals again.

"That was an impressive show you put on in there," he said, resting his shoulder against the doorframe of her tiny office.

"You too." She continued gathering the papers that were scattered across her desk, stacking them neatly in her briefcase.

"So what will you do for three days while the board members make up their minds?" he asked, picking up a paper she'd dropped.

"Research the next project." She took the sheet from him without looking up and laid it on top of the others. "Excuse me," she said, snapping the briefcase closed. "I have to go."

He made no move to clear the door. Instead, he stepped into the office, effectively blocking her exit.

What he had to say wouldn't wait for her unlikely invitation.

"Summer."

She held her briefcase in front of her like a shield. "Look," he began, "we've both made our pitches to the board, there's nothing more you can do until they make a decision."

Her gaze did not quite meet his, seeming to focus somewhere beyond him.

"Please," he said, reaching out his hands palms up, "I thought we were friends, more than that."

She stared at him, her expression composed—and as blank as a clean chalkboard. He wondered how much effort that pose took. After watching that go-for-broke presentation she'd arranged, he knew she wasn't going to forgive him for jeopardizing the project. He'd been stupid to even hope. His gaze traveled her length. She was all Humantec now, from her tightly wound hair to her tailored suit. The outfit showed her curves all right, but they weren't the soft curves he'd touched only days ago. These curves were calculated, displayed to subtle but full advantage.

She stood rigidly before him, a Humantec robot, under total control. It made him antsy. His own actions were far from controllable right now. He wanted to shake her.

"Damn," he said with a low growl of frustration. She stayed ramrod stiff, and he had to quell the urge to say something to make her flinch. It was all he could do not to smash her protective wall to smithereens. He clenched his teeth. "After all that's happened between us, can't you even try to understand my position?" He heard her sharp intake of breath.

"Your position? Oh, I think I understand. You only did what you had to do. Anything is permissible as long as it gets you your halfway house."

He saw the subtle drop of her shoulders as she answered, the barely perceptible flutter of her eyelids when she looked directly at him for a brief moment. Uncertainty, he thought. She wasn't quite the Humantec robot after all.

"Oh, I understand your position all right," she was saying, her voice as stiff as her back. "I've just been an obstacle in your path. But whatever ruthlessness you accuse Humantec of, Dr. Jericho, your methods are far worse—"

"Summer, that's not—"

"You think you can justify your lies and trickery with a noble cause—but you can't."

Her eyes were wide and shiny as they leveled on him, and he could tell she was fighting tears. It was oddly gratifying to know he was getting through to her. If only he could hold her, tuck her warm body close to his and make her realize she didn't have to protect herself from him. Why did he want that so much?

"Don't," she said when he made a move toward her.

"I care about you, Summer. Please believe that. I didn't plan what happened between us but—"

Her long, graceful fingers trembled as she touched her hand to her forehead. She shook her head. When she looked at him again, her eyes were vacant, her expression hardening into emptiness as she straightened her back.

"I have work to do," she said, her words carrying the sharp edge of dismissal.

She wasn't going to lower her guard, not now. She

stood before him with her chin up, as protected as a soldier in an armored tank—a tank called Humantec. He was certain now she would never give him a chance as long as she kept her defenses in place. He wrestled down a powerful urge to make her cry—anything to see honest emotion. But he knew she was only safeguarding herself—from him.

"Summer, I never meant to hurt you—"

"You were just doing your job." The words sounded forced as she hugged her briefcase.

"No, I wasn't just doing my job, and neither were you."

Her knuckles whitened, but the lines of her face remained rigid. Oh, how he needed to pull her into his arms, he thought as he watched her slip away from him.

"This isn't just about Humantec and Sandy Flats clinic," he said, searching for a glimmer of understanding in her shadowed gaze. "It's about people. You and me."

"Ryan, you're in my way."

When she looked past him as if he were already out of her life, something inside of him snapped. "I'm in your way?" he asked, the flame of hopeless anger burning deep. "You've got your mind conveniently and safely made up, haven't you?"

"I don't know what you're talking about," she said icily. She smoothed the already perfect bun at the nape of her neck.

The action heated him further.

"It's easy for you to declare us enemies, isn't it? We're factions at war now, not people—just a software company and a halfway house. That's how you like it.

You can't stand to be human, to trust, to feel. You know what you are, Summer Keeton? You are a coward."

Her eyes flashed to life. "What did you say?"

"You heard me. Being human means pain. That's right, pain, and along with it confusion, and somewhere in there, believe it or not, a chance for joy. Real joy, the soul-kicking, heart-stopping kind. But you don't want any of that, do you?"

Ryan's anger swept through him like a hot wind, drying his mouth, stinging his eyes. "You want to stay safe—always behind your computers, your precious Humantec land of logic." He stepped away from the door. "Then go on, Summer—go and hide."

Her face paled. For a moment, she made no move at all, standing so still, he could hardly tell she was breathing.

"Ryan Jericho," she said, pointing a shaky finger at him, "I don't need the kind of feelings you're talking about. It was a mistake for me to get involved here— with you or your kids." She turned on her heel to leave but the door was blocked by Roscoe's heavy frame.

"Uh, excuse me, Ms. Keeton," he said. "Have you seen . . . ? Oh, there you are. Ryan, I just received word one of your clients has been admitted to the emergency room. Phoebe Prescot." He looked down at the note he held in his hand.

"What happened?" asked Ryan, unceremoniously snatching the paper from him.

Roscoe continued to stare at his empty hands. "She overdosed on a narcotic of some kind—probable suicide attempt."

Summer put her hand to her mouth. "Oh no."

"She's in intensive care." Roscoe plunged his hands in his pockets. "The family's been notified."

"I'm going directly to the hospital," said Ryan.

He couldn't believe it. Suicide? No. Not Phoebe. His heartbeat throbbed at his temples. But he'd been wrong before. Dead wrong.

He heard footsteps behind him as he strode down the hall, but he didn't slow his pace. His thoughts were shrouded in a dark fog. Vaguely, he registered the sound as it faded.

The air in the hospital waiting room was heavy with the smell of antiseptic. Summer forced tiny gulps of it into her tight lungs, unable to catch her breath. Jimmy Prescot had fixed his stare on the television set while Ryan talked to him in earnest tones, his voice too low for her to hear from across the room. Summer stayed where she was.

She was useless, paralyzed by the dread that had seized her the moment she entered the hospital. It was unreasonable, but it was as real as the thick air she was trying to breathe. She was suffocating in the grip of a terrifying beast. In a cold, sterile room just like this one, she had learned her mother was dead. And now it was Phoebe whose fate she awaited.

No matter what Ryan said, she knew Phoebe would not have run away, would not have ended up here if it hadn't been for her meddling. It had taken all the nerve she could muster to step through the hospital doors. But she'd had to come.

If only Ryan would talk to her, his soothing voice, his gentle words would surely loosen the steel band around her chest. No, she couldn't let herself think that way. He wasn't there for her.

Thankfully, he had not cast her a glance since she'd arrived. Needing his attention at a time like this made her feel even worse. She shouldn't want him so. He was busy with Jimmy, giving him the support he so desperately needed. That was where he was supposed to be. She didn't need him, she didn't want him. She sat still, keeping her muscles from betraying her frantic thoughts, fighting her panic alone and wondering if he'd been right to call her a coward.

She bit her lip, watching a young doctor approach Jimmy and Ryan. "She's going to make it," the man said quietly. She closed her eyes, letting relief wash over her as she listened to Ryan's calm voice asking for details. Phoebe is sleeping, the doctor told him, it had been close, but she would be all right.

All right, thought Summer. She smiled weakly and managed to open her eyes. She'd been desperate to leave, and now it was okay. It shamed her to know that a part of her was undeniably thankful she now had permission to go.

The doctor motioned Jimmy Prescot toward the room, telling him he could see his daughter, but only for a few minutes. Jimmy disappeared down the hall.

She could go now—just walk on out of there. She looked at Ryan who sat bent over, intent on some obscure speck on the floor. No, she wasn't going to leave. There was no running away from the fears that plagued her. She needed to talk to Ryan to explain.

Summer stood, cursing her wobbly legs, and made her way across the room. She touched his shoulder as she took Jimmy's place beside him. He gave an almost imperceptible shrug. She let her hand drop.

"I should have seen it coming," he mumbled, half to himself. His face was drawn. "I was so sure Phoebe wasn't taking drugs . . . damn." He clenched his fists. "I should have left this place months ago."

Her heart twisted at the pain etched into his face. "You don't know what you're saying, Ryan."

"Oh, but I do." His eyes were haunted.

"It's my fault," she said. "I should have stopped her from running away."

"No, Summer." He took her by the shoulders. His touch was rough, not at all comforting. "You could not have stopped her from leaving. She was my client, I misjudged—" He let her go abruptly and turned away. "Hell, maybe nobody could've stopped her." His voice trailed to a whisper. "I was so sure she wasn't suicidal . . ."

For a long time, Ryan stared at the television set. Summer took his hand and held it gently between hers, but his eyes stayed trained on the flickering screen, worlds away from her. She sensed there was something terribly wrong.

"Ryan . . ." her voice caught. "You did everything you could," she said, fighting back tears. "Phoebe will be okay." She gulped hard. "As long as she is alive, she has a chance. Maybe she's learned something now . . . maybe . . ."

"That's enough, Summer. Don't you think I know all that?" His handsome features were frozen into a harsh mask. He pulled his hand away. "Look, there's no point in you staying here any longer," he said, sounding strangely detached. "Go get some rest, you've been here long enough."

"Are you leaving?" she asked.

"No. I need to stay for Jimmy," he said in a monotone.

"Ryan, what is it? Please tell me." She waited for a long moment. He did not answer. "Trust me, Ryan, I can—"

"Trust you?" He gave a humorless laugh. "You've got it wrong, real wrong."

"But—"

"Go on, Summer, get out of here." He returned his gaze to the television set.

She hesitated, watching a tiny muscle in his jaw work back and forth. Her heart pounded against her chest. He's shutting you out, she thought as she made her way to the exit, not looking back. And you're letting him.

You are a coward, Summer Keeton.

Bright sunlight beamed through the lacy bedroom curtains. Summer squinted against it from her nest under the covers, wishing she could sleep until it was dark again. But her body was too attuned to early rising to give her that peace.

With effort, she rolled over to check her travel alarm clock. It glowed a faint 10:00 A.M. Not nearly late enough. She considered pulling the blankets over her head but her back was beginning to ache from the unaccustomed hours in bed.

She couldn't stay locked up in this little room forever, no matter how much she wanted to. She thought of Ryan's face, not how it had looked in the hospital, but in the swamp, dripping wet and so close to hers, she could feel the heat of his skin, how warm and insistent his lips had felt when he'd kissed her that first time. Her chest tightened. When she was with him, the very air seemed vibrant, teeming with possibilities. He'd given her so much, unlocking a part of her that she never knew existed. No, she couldn't think about that anymore.

She wished she could go to the clinic and work on the system. Do something, anything to fill the emptiness. It had gnawed at her incessantly since she'd left the hospital yesterday. But the board suspended work on Humantec's project until they made a decision, leaving her with no diversion from the miserable mess she'd made of things. The knowledge weighed on her, making every thought difficult, every movement sluggish.

She struggled to sit up, the movement jolting her more awake than she wanted to be. And then she remembered Max. She'd been so busy trying to salvage the project, she'd forgotten to call him. He'd be back in Atlanta by now. Holding on to the thought like a lifeline, she mustered the energy to pull herself out of bed.

Max. What would he say? She waited for the usual tension to take hold and spur her into action. But it didn't come. No familiar blast of adrenaline quickened her heart rate. No flow of excitement heated her blood. So what would Max think?

She sat on the edge of her bed, her concern for Max's opinion sliding away from her like icing on a warm cake. What if she didn't complete the installation? It was only a business deal. No one would die over it.

The thought tightened her throat. She never worried about death when she worked with her computers. Computers didn't live or die, they were just there, running on predictable little electrical impulses that switched on and off according to precise, controllable codes.

Oh how she needed to get back to those machines.

Maybe Max had closed the deal in Bombay. That would mean immediate work for her. He seemed certain of it the last time he'd called. If he'd gotten the contract, Sandy Flats wouldn't be quite so important now, would it? If the project was as big as he'd hinted, they could even pull out of Sandy Flats now, cut their losses. Maybe they wouldn't even wait for the board's decision.

She lifted her tangled hair out of her eyes, not quite believing the direction of her thoughts. Pull out now? Chicken-heart.

But there it was. Sandy Flats wasn't just a computer installation anymore. Somehow she'd gotten involved. This place was full of real people with real problems. Too real. She had to get as far away from it as possible. She wasn't doing anyone any good anyway. She couldn't even talk to Ryan.

What had happened to him at the hospital? He'd said something about leaving. No, that couldn't have been it. *You can't do anything about that anyway. You tried, he doesn't want you around. He doesn't want you.*

Her stomach twisted, and she pressed her palms tightly to her eyes. She wasn't going to let him do this to her. She couldn't, it hurt too much.

He manipulated you, she reminded herself, trying to catch hold of the anger she'd felt before, that made it easier. *He played a game with you, a game to get what he wanted.*

Slowly she picked up her terry cloth robe from the foot of the bed and wrapped herself in its dull green. The soft cream walls of her room looked stark in the harsh morning light and seemed to close in on her. She pulled the ties of the robe tight. What had happened to the warm cream-puff welcome she'd once felt in this room?

She traced a pattern on the rug with her foot, and her emptiness grew. Ryan's attention was just a part of his deception, she told herself. His caresses were only a means to an end. And the warmth . . . the warmth she felt at his touch, that was the biggest lie of all.

But it wasn't.

No, she couldn't make herself believe that—no matter how hard she tried. She'd seen his eyes at the hospital, staring within. He didn't play games. Ryan cared.

How could she condemn him? He was suffering now, more than she could ever imagine. He couldn't lock away his feelings the way she could. He poured his heart and soul into other people's lives, felt their anguish and joy as his own. Whatever Ryan Jericho had done, he'd done it selflessly, to help the kids, not to hurt her. And there was nothing she could do about that. She couldn't even bring herself to talk to him.

If only she could get away from Sandy Flats. To stay any longer was dangerous. She was certain of that. And poor Phoebe had suffered the worst for her misbegotten interest. She clenched her fists. No matter what

Ryan said, she felt responsible for Phoebe. If she'd only known what to say, what to do, that night Phoebe had run away. If only the girl had had somewhere else to go.

She shook her head to clear it. Somewhere else to go. Ryan was right. He'd been right all along, and she'd been too wrapped up in Humantec to understand. She stood up and paced across the floor, the faint tug of a newborn idea fueling her movements. Back and forth she walked.

"I'll straighten this mess out," she said aloud, the words sealing her decision. She owed it to Phoebe. And she owed it to Ryan.

So what if she wasn't warm and caring. She couldn't be, she had to be tough, and she had to leave Sandy Flats to stay that way. But she could fix her mistake. She'd convince Max to work with her on this one, she'd have to. Squaring her shoulders, she marched down the hall toward the shower, her determination growing with each step.

Warm water cascaded down her back as she considered plan after plan—rejecting one, then another, until she was satisfied she had one that would work. By the time the water ran cold, she knew exactly what she would say when she called Max.

"So when can we go to India? You all finished with Sandy Flats?" he asked, before she'd even had a chance to say hello. "We've both got to do the preliminary site visit. This is the biggest deal yet. We'll need—"

"Max," she said loudly, interrupting his excited flow. She waited a moment for the line to go quiet, then spoke in calm, even tones. "I have an idea."

"Great!" he said. "Listen, we're going to need to

add a few frills and thrills to the system for these guys, punch it up a bit. I'll let you know the details—"

"Max, there is a problem here. A very big problem." That should get his attention. She waited another moment to let it sink in. She had to control the pace of this conversation. Max would listen to her when he knew it was important. "Maxwell Pelion, you should have told me about the contract change."

"What? Oh . . . I know. But, Summer, I didn't think it would make any difference. You always work like a demon anyway. I knew you'd get things set up just like usual. . . ." He paused. "You did, didn't you?"

"No." She let the silence float down heavily. His attention was fully hers now.

She told him about the presentation to the board members, omitting a few details. She didn't want to discuss Ryan Jericho, not with Max, not with anybody. She also didn't tell him about Phoebe. This was her problem, and she was going to take care of it, for her own reasons.

Instead, she outlined her plan, making sure Max saw how much it would benefit Humantec. When she finished, she listened to the faint crackle across the phone line. "Max? Are you still there?"

"You aren't giving us much time to negotiate here."

"Now, Max, you're the one who's always wanting to jump in with both feet. I'm just telling you where to jump this time." She held her breath, hoping she hadn't gone too far. Dealing with the business side of Max took a bit of bravado.

"Summer, this wasn't in the original plan—"

"Of course not, but when I see an opportunity, I

think it should be explored. Are you up to it, Max?"
She heard his exhale.

"You have thought this out, haven't you, in detail?"

Sure she had, as much as it took for this phone call.
"Come on, Max. You're talking to Summer Keeton.
What do you think?"

"I have to admit, it does have possibilities."

She could almost see him grin; Max loved a challenge. "With this kind of software, we need to test extensively in a working clinic," she said. "We'll let Sandy Flats use it to create treatment plans and then keep a data base to monitor progress. I'll design the system for flexible tailoring step-by-step. That's our selling edge. We'll program for Sandy Flats and everybody else at the same time."

Max chuckled. "Roscoe Williams and I hit it off pretty well when I was down there before. I'll get on the phone and see what I can cook up," he said. "Roscoe was our big supporter when I sold the system. If I can convince him, I think we can work something out."

"I'm sure you can," said Summer, satisfied that his natural enthusiasm for business dealings had taken over. If Max liked an idea, he could make it work. It was a gift of sorts, and it had helped Humantec immensely.

"He'll go for it," Max was saying, his speech speeding up along with his enthusiasm. "It's a dream of a deal. I'd been hoping you'd want to expand the system, Summer. But you liked being on the road so much, I wasn't sure you'd go for designing again."

"What?" She felt her jaw drop.

"But I want you in Bombay as soon as possible."

She picked at her robe, still damp from her shower,

listening to his words gather momentum, leaving her
behind. He hadn't even known she wanted to redesign
the system. He thought she enjoyed being on the road.

"Sure, Max," she said automatically when he paused
to take a breath.

"As soon as we've got confirmation to use Sandy
Flats as a test site, we'll need to get to India," said Max.
"I'm booking our flights now."

Good, she thought, fighting the sadness that
descended like a thick, suffocating blanket. Saying
good-bye in a daze, she hung up the phone, feeling her
energy dip as their link was severed. She shook her
head. Had she been so remote that her own partner
didn't know her? Maybe there were a few things she
ought to change.

She sighed deeply, wiping at an unexpected tear
with the back of her hand. At least now Ryan would get
his halfway house. Stoically she blinked the rest of her
tears back and opened the armoire, staring at the familiar row of neutral-hued suits hanging in a neat row.
Their monotones, once so comforting, sent an uneasiness prickling across her skin. It was as if her life hung
in that closet, musty and stale. She closed the door.

"I'm doing all I can," she said to the empty room.
She pulled a thin cotton blouse and a pair of loose-
fitting white pants from the dresser. "I can't do any
more. I can't."

She had to leave this town as soon as possible—
repair and retreat. It was the only logical course. She
dressed quickly, conscious of a disconcerting feeling
that someone was scowling at her. I need to get out of
here, she decided as she haphazardly braided her hair.

━━━◈━━━━━━━━━◈━━━

Shading her eyes against the sun's glare, Summer stood among the flowers in Carrie Alford's garden, watching the bleached white sky. Trickles of sweat crawled like ants beneath her dampening blouse. The air, thick and gardenia sweet, seemed to close in around her.

She had a plan, a good plan, so why did she feel so uncertain? "What's wrong with me?" she said into the heavy silence.

The answer was everywhere she turned, everywhere she saw Ryan's image framed by brilliant flowers. But his face was different. His laughing eyes were dull and focused inward, his teasing grin faded into a grim line.

Summer closed her eyes and felt sadness loom over her like a great cowardly bird. It was wrong to let Ryan get so close, wrong to start to care. No one could make his pain go away, least of all her. She swayed slightly, and a strong hand steadied her. Ryan? She felt a thrill that died as she looked up.

"Hold on there, missy," said Marcus, his dark face close to hers. "You're about to tumble headfirst into those daylilies." As he studied her, his face wrinkled in concern. "You okay?"

"Yes, of course. I . . . I was looking for storm clouds."

"You feel it too? This heat's building. Air's thick enough to float a catfish." He demonstrated with a labored breath. "Storm's comin' for sure."

Carrie Alford glided silently through the gardenia hedge. Her appearance from nowhere always startled

Summer. It was as if the woman was one of the garden spirits herself.

"Summer dear," she said in her high bird-voice, brushing her fingertips lightly across Summer's cheek. "Lovely flower." Her lips smiled, but her eyes penetrated. "You're so pale today. Are you drifting away from us?"

"I'll be leaving soon."

"I see."

The woman's intense blue gaze, so like Ryan's, held hers, making her feel as if her innermost thoughts were being probed.

"Girl's been out in this heat too long," said Marcus, his matter-of-fact tone breaking the strange moment.

"Come, Summer one," Carrie said, hooking her arm through Summer's. "It's cooler by the water. We should talk now." The voice was gentle, but the command clear.

"Mind the sky," said Marcus after them.

Carrie sat down on the edge of the dock with surprising nimbleness, her tiny feet dangling inches above the water. "Ryan called this morning," she said as she motioned to Summer to sit beside her. "He told me about Phoebe."

"Oh." Was Ryan all right? How did he sound? Her lips closed over the questions. "I'm so sorry this had to happen. Ryan was at the hospital when I left but I—" Her words caught in her throat. She licked her lips and stared at the dark water.

"Dear girl." A knowing smile creased Carrie's wrinkled face. "You do care about him, don't you?"

She tried to shrug but her shoulders quivered oddly instead.

Carrie was silent for a moment, watching her with large considering eyes. "I believe you can help him," she said softly.

Somewhere close by a fish slapped its tail against the surface of the water, magnifying the stillness of the swamp.

"All I've done so far is cause trouble," said Summer, swallowing hard.

The old woman shook her head.

"No, Carrie, it's true." Summer tried explaining about the halfway house and how Ryan had tried to stop Humantec's project and how she'd befriended Phoebe, all of it tumbling out in a disorganized jumble. But Carrie simply looked at her as if she already knew these things.

"I can at least fix some of the mess I made," said Summer, pleading for understanding. "I've come up with an idea for enhancing Humantec's system that will save the halfway house."

Carrie gave her an indulgent smile.

"We'll automate treatment plans and provide patient success monitoring. I'll add some statistical functions and a projection program too," Summer told her in a rush, like air suddenly escaping from a balloon. "The hospital in Bombay will love these enhancements, but they're too big to use for testing. Sandy Flats is perfect—small enough to monitor and correct problems quickly, big enough to use all the functions.

"Don't you see? With Sandy Flats as the development site, they'll have the software and Bombay will pay for it. The halfway house can keep its funding." She prayed for some sign of agreement, but Carrie only listened—with an unnerving stillness.

"I know I've caused a lot of problems," said Summer. "But I'm going to make things right."

It was a long time before Carrie spoke. When she did, her odd question took Summer by surprise.

"How much has Ryan told you about his sister?" she asked, putting a delicate hand on Summer's arm.

"He told me most of it. How he and Alicia would explore this swamp together. How he used to try to keep her out of trouble and"—Summer looked down at the dark water—"and how she died. Ryan must have loved his sister very much."

"Ah yes," said Carrie slowly. "Alicia was a beautiful child. Beautiful and capricious." A hint of sadness misted her voice. "When she grew up, the games became more serious, and she would not always allow her guardian to play." She dug into her skirt pocket and pulled out a small tapestried purse. Searching through it, she produced a photograph of a young girl.

"Alicia?"

"Yes," Carrie said, handing her the picture.

The girl was standing on the front steps of Alford Place, wearing a frilly gown and carrying a parasol. Summer could see by her coloring that she was Ryan's flesh and blood. Black hair and ice-blue eyes. But where Ryan exuded power and strength, the young woman in the picture portrayed a crystalline delicacy, infinitely breakable. She was small, with rounded hips, a tiny waist, and a rosebud mouth. An old-fashioned beauty that begged to be cared for, tended like a hothouse lily.

"She's beautiful," said Summer.

"Alicia had been traveling with her mother for several years. We didn't know there were serious problems. The letters Ryan received from his mother and father were vague." Carrie paused. "And there were none from Alicia."

Arranging the folds of her dress in slow, meticulous movements, Carrie looked out over the water. "Alicia had become secretive, expertly so. Even her parents didn't understand how bad it was. She left to come back to the States. I think she expected Ryan to fix things, just like he always had for her. But he couldn't, not this time."

She took the photograph back, not looking at the girl in the picture. "We didn't find out until afterward that she'd been hospitalized when she returned to this country. She was on medication when she came here to us."

Sweet Alicia, so beautiful, so vulnerable, thought Summer, watching Carrie gently tuck the picture back into her skirt pocket.

"Ryan blames himself for her death," said Carrie.

He would, thought Summer, he would take on that pain. She gripped the edge of the dock. That was what she'd seen in his eyes at the hospital.

"Ryan needs your help," Carrie said softly.

Summer held her breath. Her gaze followed Carrie's to a crane wading the shallows for a meal. The heat of the morning seemed to increase, the thick air weighing heavily on her shoulders. "I don't know if I—"

"Do what is in your heart," she said.

"But—"

Carrie stood, cutting her off with a motion of her hand. "Your heart, Summer one."

Dark currents eddied around the dock's pilings. Summer surveyed the expanse of water stretching before her. Prescot's Landing was upriver, the direction she and Ryan had taken that hot afternoon not so long ago.

Carrie's words rang in her head as her gaze traveled downriver. She could find his cottage easily. He'd said only a few miles separated them by canoe. She couldn't change what had happened, but she could go to him. The river lapped at the edge of the dock in a quiet plea. Ryan needed her. Aiming the canoe in the direction of the cottage, she used the paddle as a rudder to steer the craft into the center of the river where the current silently accommodated her urgency, grabbing the craft and pushing it along.

In spite of the river's help, Summer's skin was soon damp with the effort it took to keep the canoe from veering into sandbars and fallen trees. The thin fabric of her blouse clung to her in the moist heat. Gathering her shirttails, she tied them around her waist, and kicked off her sandals, grateful for the feel of cool metal beneath her feet.

She followed the meander of the current, maneuvering the canoe back and forth, Carrie's words filling her mind. The soft, twittering voice sang in her ears, insisting she look into the one place she'd avoided with all her being.

With her paddle poised in midair, the canoe drifting with the slow-moving water, it came to her. Revealed like a flower unfolding each dewy petal to the morning sun, Summer discovered what was in her heart. She knew then that what she felt for Ryan Jericho was love.

It wasn't safe. It wasn't reasonable. It was love. He hadn't been completely honest with her, but he hadn't lied, had he? And he'd tricked her only as much as she was willing to be tricked. She'd deceived herself by seeing no farther than the secure world of her computer screen.

Love—yes, she loved him.

She leaned into her strokes, making them strong and even, feeling an impatient force that drove her on. She would give Ryan whatever solace she could. He didn't have to be alone . . . and neither did she.

The river narrowed into an overgrown channel, its banks melting into a steamy tangle of vegetation. She couldn't see solid ground now, only thick cypress trunks and tight clumps of swamp grass. A cloud crossing the sun cut the heat and plunged her into cool shadow. She looked up. The sky had darkened to a menacing gray-brown.

The usual steady buzz of insects ceased, giving way to an unnatural silence. Still air surrounded her, pressing its weight against her chest as the lush, life-giving swamp held its breath, expectant and dangerous.

She plunged the paddle into the dark water, its splash echoing in the eerie quiet. The canoe slid out of the narrow channel and into a sandbar. Cursing under her breath, Summer dug the paddle's tip into its mushy softness. With a frustrated push, she tried to turn the canoe aside. The sand sucked greedily at her paddle, and she grit her teeth, yanking it out.

As the wind picked up, unpredictable gusts made it a continuous struggle to stay in the river's center. Ryan's cottage had to be close. But could she make it there before the storm broke? Her muscles ached as she pulled harder with each stroke, determined to try.

Strands of hair escaped her braid and whipped across her face, mimicking the moss that waved in the trees around her. She pushed the tangle back with her forearm, unwilling to let go of the paddle, her only weapon against the force of the wind. The action blinded her just as a gust smashed furiously into the canoe, scooting it sideways under a low branch. She ducked, holding her paddle in front of her to ward it off. When she straightened up, her heart stopped.

Coiled around the paddle's handle, inches from where her sweating fingers gripped the smooth wood, a water moccasin flicked its split tongue at her.

It drew back, hissing a clear warning.

Summer dropped the paddle and scrambled backward. The snake lunged. Grabbing the branch above, she frantically dodged the attack while the canoe drifted out from under her.

She hung helplessly above the water, trying to gather her wits. The snake was nowhere in sight and the canoe, traveling along with the current, was drifting farther and farther away from her.

She had to get it.

Taking a shaky breath, she let go of the branch, dropping with a small splash into the cool, dark water. Swimming with adrenaline-enhanced strokes, she gained swiftly on the escaping canoe. Just as she reached up to grab the gunwale, the snake slithered over the side.

Madly, she frog-kicked backward, staring at the black ripple coming toward her. Her heart pumped hard against her chest as it drew steadily closer. She held her breath, ready to duck under, but at the last minute, the creature veered off and swam past. With a deep gasp, she let it out and watched the empty canoe round the next bend without a hitch.

And it began to rain.

Slipping on the mushy ground, she climbed out of the water and hugged herself against the chill of the wind as she studied the gloom ahead. She'd just follow the river to the cottage.

"I'll be there in no time," she said aloud to bolster her confidence. Her dripping body answered in a paroxysm of shivers.

She took a step forward and sank several inches into the spongy peat. All right, so it would be slow going. She'd either have to trudge through this muck or swim. One look back at the river, now dotted with rain circles, convinced her not to take any more chances with snakes.

The mud and dense undergrowth made progress a slow struggle, leaving no time for any thought other than how to avoid the vines that wound mercilessly back and forth across her path. She forced herself on, slipping and sliding, dodging the limbs that grabbed at her hair with strong, knobby fingers.

Time had stilled, and Summer felt like she'd been in the swamp for an eternity when she spotted a clearing ahead. She headed toward it at a slow jog, thinking she'd reached the cottage. But as soon as she picked up speed she tripped over a root, stumbling clumsily forward and crashing headlong into a fat cypress trunk.

Eyes shut, she lay still for a moment, sprawled facedown in green slime. When she lifted her head to spit out a mouthful of peat, an unsteadying sensation of nausea swept through her. She closed her eyes again, too dizzy to try to stand. Curling up, she hugged her knees and bent her head against the hard pounding of the rain.

NINE

Ryan woke to the persistent slamming of a door. He sat up on the sofa, trying to orient himself, his groggy mind resisting mightily.

Swamp Monster placed a paw on his jean-clad knee and whined.

"Don't give me your Lassie routine, big boy. I'm not in the mood," Ryan mumbled, ruffing the dog's scruffy head. "What a night." He leaned back and rested his forearm over his eyes, ignoring Monster's repeated nosing.

He'd stayed up with Jimmy until dawn, mainly to keep him from getting his gun and going after Speedy. He'd only been able to see Phoebe for a few moments. She was weak and frighteningly pale, still too confused to talk to him. For the first time in his career, he was almost glad he couldn't communicate with a client. It was unprofessional, but he'd kept seeing Alicia's small, round face against the pillow. That horrible death mask had frozen him on the spot. Hell of a way for a therapist to react.

But he was taking care of that. He'd been invited to join a research team, the offer from the University of North Carolina had been in the mail two days ago. He was going to accept it whether Sandy Flats had a halfway house or not.

The slam of the door was making his head ache. The rattle of rusted hinges grated on his raw nerves.

What had he missed with Phoebe? His mind, still half asleep, wouldn't tune into it clearly. The girl had not seemed suicidal to him, he simply hadn't seen it. She was angry all right, but not despondent. He shook his throbbing head.

The door slammed again, this time with enough violence to compel him into action. He stumbled out the back door toward the annoying sound and blinked in slow-witted surprise at the storm that was suddenly raging around him.

The rain blew through the screen and soaked his shirtless chest in seconds. It revived his foggy brain. With a swift movement, he grabbed the porch door that had been swinging against the house and pulled it shut, securing its latch against the wind.

He stayed on the porch, breathing huge gulps of the wet air until his head began to clear. He'd listened to Jimmy Prescot vent his anger all night. "It's that boyfriend of hers," Jimmy told him over and over, "ought to be after him now."

Ryan groaned. How well he understood the man's frustration, and the futility of his fight. Nothing Jimmy Prescot could do to Phoebe's boyfriend would give him the daughter he wanted. The fact that Jimmy cared so much was making things worse. He swore under his breath. Hadn't he just found that out with Summer?

Rain trickled down his face. She was probably right to cut off the feelings that made life confusing. He wiped the water out of his eyes.

He should have known it, too, especially after Alicia. How could he keep making the same mistakes over and over? He slumped into a rickety, ladder-back chair, letting the chill of the rain sink into his bones. Monster put a wet nose to his hand and whined. Absently he scratched the dog behind the ears and stared into the storm.

After Alicia killed herself he'd made his decision to give up counseling. He should've left the clinic months ago. Only he'd kept finding reasons to stay. The halfway house was the last. He was clearly doing more harm than good now. The thought shook him.

How could he go on, knowing he'd been so blind? It was torture to let go of the thing he did best, but he knew he had to. The halfway house had given focus to his energy, had helped keep it from deteriorating into self-loathing.

He tilted the chair back until it rested against the wooden planks of the cottage and closed his eyes. Was there no end to the damage he could do?

A crack of thunder echoed through the swamp, punctuating his wretchedness. Only the rain commiserated as it dripped steadily from the sagging eaves.

Monster whined.

He could hear the dog's claws clicking on the rough boards of the porch as he paced back and forth. Opening his eyes a bare slit, Ryan looked down. A furry muzzle nudged his leg. "What is it, pal? You can't want to go out in this mess." He glanced toward the windswept water. Every muscle in his body tensed at what he saw.

He squinted to see through the rain as the empty canoe drifted swiftly downriver.

By the time he reached the dock, there was little doubt in his mind where the craft had come from. He grabbed the anchor that lay in the bottom of his fishing boat and tossed it into the canoe. Holding on to the opposite end of the anchor rope, he pulled steadily, guiding the canoe up to the dock.

It was Aunt Carrie's boat. There was no paddle, only a pair of sandals floating in a half inch of water. Summer's? They had to be. Straining his gaze upriver, he could see only a heavy curtain of gray-green rain.

He wasted no time mooring the canoe and hopping into his fishing boat. He called to Swamp Monster, but the dog was crashing through the brush along the river. "Stupid animal," he shouted, needing someone to yell at.

Aiming the boat upriver, he searched the banks for signs of her, heedless of the tempest surrounding him. He watched the black water as well, his heart frozen against the fear of what he might find. Please Lord, not that.

The river switched right and then back left. He slowed the boat, almost choking the motor, painstakingly guiding it around a tree that had blown into the water. Anxiously, he peered into the mist ahead, seeing nothing but the next bend in the river.

As if to defy his determination, the storm intensified. Ryan squinted against bullets of rain, steering his boat closer to the bank as the wind whipped around him, howling in his ears.

Howling? That wasn't the wind, it was Swamp Monster. The dog sounded like a hound treeing a raccoon. Or maybe . . . he nosed the boat into the bank and threw the anchor ashore. "Monster!" he called. "Here, boy . . . Monster! Where are you?"

The dog didn't appear. Should he chance a wild-goose chase into the woods? Would he miss something upriver? He was frantic with worry and in no mood to stand in the rain calling a fool dog.

The howling started again, closer now. He jumped into the shallows and hauled the boat a few feet onto the muddy bank. Pushing through a waist-high patch of ferns, he hurried toward Monster's eerie call. "You'd better know what you're bellowing about, dog," he muttered grimly.

He found her huddled against a cypress tree, be-draggled and shivering, her face as pale as moonlight—the most beautiful sight in the world. And then she was in his arms, soft and sobbing. He crushed her to him until he felt his heart start beating again.

Summer buried her face in Ryan's warm, damp chest. She felt herself being lifted and then carried. "I . . . I'm all right," she said, making no move to un-wrap her arms from his neck.

"Oh? Then what are you doing out here in the swamp in this storm?" he demanded, his voice raspy and harsh.

She felt foolish, chastised by his sudden gruffness. "I was . . . just out in the canoe and . . . I saw a snake and I . . . fell out . . . I was trying to . . ." She stopped, her courage draining away like the rivulets of water streaming through his dark hair.

Just wait, she told herself, the middle of a storm is no place to declare your love, especially when the ob-ject of that love is scowling at you so. She rested her head against his shoulder, trying to think of how she should present her discovery, but the strong, steady pounding of his heart crowded her thoughts.

Her awareness narrowed to the feel of Ryan's shoulder against her cheek, the warmth in the strong arms that held her. Even when he had deposited her safely beside him on the cold metal seat of the boat, she felt wrapped securely in his protection.

"Thank you for finding me," she said, suddenly shy. "I can always rely on you."

"No, Summer, you can't." He stared at the river in front of them.

The ice in his tone made her shiver. "Are . . . Are you all right?" she asked, knowing he wasn't at all.

"Yes." His reply was curt, a warning not to press further.

As the rain fell, she felt her newfound resolve melting beneath its steady pound. She stared at the river ahead. What could she do? There was no computer manual to open and study, no logical rules to follow, nothing to guide her safely through her task. How do you tell a man you love him? Her eyes misted with rain and tears. She was in a new land now, with no idea how to proceed.

Ryan moored the boat at his dock, continuing his silence. Chewing her lip, Summer stepped onto the dock and watched him. His tanned cheek was shadowed with whiskers, his damp hair curled down his neck. A profound tenderness welled inside her, boosting her waning courage.

"I came to see you," she blurted out clumsily.

"Oh?" He didn't look up from lashing the bowline.

"I mean, I wasn't just, ah, out paddling around."

"Hard to do without a paddle." The mask of his face was readable only in the darkness of the blue gaze that settled on her.

"I tried to explain. There was a snake and—"

"Not now. You need to get into some dry clothes. I'll take you back to Alford—"

"No, Ryan." She pulled at a dripping strand of her hair. "Don't you even want to know why I'm here?"

"Because Monster has a good nose and found you out in the swamp." He grabbed both her shoulders hard. "Summer, don't you know you could have been killed?"

I love you, she wanted to say, but the man standing before her was a stranger. The wind whipped about them like an angry beast as their eyes met. For a long moment, Summer was oblivious to the fury raging around her, focusing only on the storm within the man she loved. She was suddenly very frightened for him, and for herself.

"Summer, you shouldn't have come." He was shouting to be heard above the sounds of wind and rain.

"But I'm here now and—"

Lightning struck a nearby tree, cutting her off with a resounding crack. Swamp Monster made a mad dash from the woods, scampering up the steep stairs to the cottage.

"Let's not get fried out here arguing," said Ryan, wrapping his arm around her waist. Half pulling, half pushing, he ushered her inside behind Monster.

"Here, dry off," he said, pulling a towel from the closet. He held it out, not meeting her gaze.

She reached for it shaking, wondering if the pressure building inside her with no sign of release would crush her from the inside out. Dripping onto the hardwood floor, she was unable to do more than clutch the towel, letting the water form pools at her feet.

She knew now that her happiness was irrevocably intertwined with Ryan's. No matter how frightened and unsure she was, she could not walk away now. She had to trust her love and she had to trust Ryan to accept it.

She shivered.

"You're getting chilled," he said, taking the towel, his movements slowing as he wrapped it securely around her body. His hands lingered, burning into her as if he were savoring the contact.

"Thank you," she said, breathless. "I . . . I'm a mess." She was shivering harder now, as much from his nearness as the rain-cooled air.

He pulled another towel from the closet and covered her dripping hair.

"You are a lot of things, Summer, but a mess is not one of them," he said, softly, looking at her with such dark sadness, she instinctively reached out from under her towel tent, putting a hand on his rough cheek.

"Ryan, I—"

"You need to dry off," he said, rubbing her hair with the towel.

Summer's throat constricted. Try as she might, the words she so longed to say would not come.

Ryan untangled the remnants of her bedraggled braid, letting the damp strands slide through his fingers, spreading them across her shoulders.

"You're beautiful," he murmured, so low, she wondered if he'd said anything at all. His warm body pressed close, heating her despite her wet clothes.

The pressure deep inside her gave way little by little as her lips sought his, each kiss, each caress, loosening the stranglehold of her newfound feelings. Her mind drifted, slipping into the sensations created by his hands as they moved over her damp skin.

She knew now she was no longer alone in the world. Ryan's touch had found her heart and his caring had unlocked it.

"Oh, Ryan." She was bursting with the need to make him understand, "Ryan, I lov—"

"You need to get out of those wet clothes," he said, pulling away woodenly. "I'd better take you back to Alford Place."

She took a deep breath, her body still trembling from his touch. "Ryan, Carrie told me about your sister. She—"

"I imagined she would, eventually. Look, Summer, she means well but—"

"Please listen, Ryan, I—"

He put his hand up, shaking his head. "Summer, don't. I'm not who or what you think I am. It's better if you go now—better for both of us." He pulled the towel around her and then dropped his hands as if forcing himself to let go. He walked stiffly to the window and stared out at the storm, his back to her.

He'd closed off from her, just like he had at the hospital. She felt her heart thumping hard and fast inside her chest. She needed to calm down, to think of a way to get through to him. There had to be one, she'd just have to figure it out. All she needed was a plan, a step-by-step logical plan. Reasonable enough. And some time.

"Ryan, do you mind if I change into something dry before we go? I'm so cold." She made her teeth chatter.

"Alford Place isn't that far away." His mouth worked, as if he wanted to say something else.

She faked a shiver. It wasn't too difficult with the butterflies beating around in her stomach.

"I'm sorry," he mumbled, rubbing his face as if trying to wake up. "This is crazy, of course I can get you something dry to wear."

"Anything will do," she said quickly. "And I think if I take a shower, I'll warm up just fine." She skittered into the bathroom before he could object. Ten minutes, that's all she'd need. She had always worked best under pressure.

The latch clicked, and Ryan gave a low groan. Good, Summer, lock yourself away from me. He couldn't trust himself with the urges that took over his mind and body when he looked at her. Touching her had been sheer torment. He hadn't meant to kiss her, and he knew he couldn't do it again, not when he was so close to the edge. As long as she was here, the world didn't seem quite so dark. And that was dangerous. He wanted her too much right now. No, he would drive her straight back to Alford Place.

It wouldn't take much for him to pull her into this mire with him. Encouraging her to get involved here in Sandy Flats had been a mistake from the beginning. She'd taken on Phoebe's problems as if they were her own, and he was the one who'd set it all up. He'd chipped away at her defenses, making her all too vulnerable.

Remembering the way she'd looked at him in the boat made his muscles tighten. The image of her rain-soaked body huddled against him as if he alone could protect her was more than he could take. He let out a short laugh. It had been sheer luck he'd found her. Luck and Swamp Monster's unerring nose.

He sank onto the sofa. Monster curled up on the floor, resting a furry paw on his foot. "You like her, too, don't you, old boy? But we have to let her go." He looked at the bathroom door. "We have no choice." Picking up a towel, he started drying off.

He could no more take care of Summer than he could stop the storm or help Alicia or Phoebe. She was better off with her armor intact.

"Damn." He hurled the towel against the wall.

Ryan was in the bedroom, searching through the dresser for something suitable for Summer to wear, when he heard the shower stop. He pulled out a flannel shirt but shoved it back. The soft green was too close to the color of Summer's eyes. This was difficult enough already, he didn't need to add to his trouble. He settled on a bulky black sweatshirt and a pair of sweatpants.

Shoving the drawer closed, he heard the pad of bare feet on wood behind him. He turned around and the beat of his heart altered painfully.

Summer stood beside the window, looking like a mythical deity in the pale, rain-washed light. Her towel was draped loosely over her curves and as he watched, she let it slip down, slowly, tantalizingly, then drop away. Entranced, he stood very still, watching her every move. The shadows of raindrops on the windowpane rippled across her body in a hypnotic dance. He swallowed hard as she stepped toward him.

"Summer, I—" He held out the sweatshirt, and she

took it away from him, tossing it on the bed with a strange beckoning smile on her lips.

"Don't say a word, Ryan." She kissed him, her naked body moving enticingly against his, silky smooth and scalding. "You should get out of these damp pants," she said, running her fingers lightly down his bare chest, heating his skin. She stopped at the waistband of his jeans.

He heard the snap and the faint noise of his zipper. Her damp hair smelled of shampoo, and he buried his face in it, not wanting to think, knowing he had to, he had to keep his senses in check. "Summer . . . Summer. What are you doing?"

"You have to ask?" she mumbled.

He cupped her face in his hands and tilted it up to him, his mind spinning as he fell into her smoldering emerald gaze. He had to make her stop, before it was too late. "Summer, this is . . . You need to—"

"Touch you," she said.

He took a sharp breath when her hand curled around him.

The wildfire she'd started deep inside him threatened to char his will to resist beyond recognition. "Do you know what you're doing?" he asked, his voice husky.

She chuckled. "Oh yes. I believe I do."

"But—"

"You talk too much, Dr. Jericho." She stroked him gently, and his ability to reason dissolved into a low groan.

He pulled her against him, his hands kneading the smooth, damp skin of her back. "Summer, I—"

Her mouth found his, her lips hot and begging.

He picked her up and laid her gently on the bed and then he drew back to look at her. She was beautiful, her golden curls spread wildly across the pillow. And she was watching him with such honest pleasure, he felt as if he would explode. He let his jeans slip to the floor with a soft thud and stretched out on the bed beside her. This was the Summer Keeton he'd been searching for all these weeks.

He circled first one lovely, firm breast with his fingertip and then the other. She moaned softly when he followed the same path with his tongue, stopping at each pink nipple to suck it erect.

"Oh, Ryan . . . Ryan." She pulled him down to her, spreading her legs so that his hardness rested in the valley between them.

Using all the control he had, he moved away.

"But, Ryan—"

"Shhh . . ." he whispered. "Only for a moment."

He pulled a tiny square packet from the bedside table while she watched him with a fire in her eyes that burned in tiny licks, blistering at every touch. "I'm surprised at you, Summer," he said gently as he tore it open. "Aren't you supposed to be the one who's always prepared?" He held up the condom.

Her eyes widened. "I . . . I wasn't thinking—"

"Ah, Summer, you don't know how long I've waited to hear that." He started to roll it on and felt her small, warm hands go around him, finishing the job. He throbbed in her grasp, and with soft murmurs of encouragement, she guided him to her.

Slowly, thoroughly he kissed her neck, her chin, her generous mouth. Beneath him, her slim hips rolled seductively.

He forced himself to go slow, holding back enough to move inside her with the gentleness she deserved. But she whispered into his ear, urging him on with breathless pleas that aroused him beyond thinking. He slid his hands down, cupping her buttocks, plunging deeply, penetrating to his full length. She gasped and rocked against him, sending a fire to his loins that threatened to burn quickly out of control.

They moved in a rhythmic dance that took possession of him, pulling him to an unbearable summit where he held on in timeless ecstasy.

And then the skies opened.

Summer gasped, and he scooped her up into his arms with a loud groan. Riding blindly beyond the stars, he held tight, certain he would die somewhere in deep space if he ever let her go.

Even long after he was spent, he would not release his hold, drinking in her softness like a man dying of thirst, forever imprinting the feel of her against him.

"Oh, Ryan, I love you."

Summer's throaty whisper yanked him brutally back from the oasis he had made for himself in her arms.

"No." He couldn't let her love him. He couldn't allow her to need him.

"I do love you, Ryan. It's why I came here today. Only you wouldn't listen to me." She wound a strand of his hair around her finger. "So I had to show you."

"Oh Lord, Summer." He felt like the worst kind of traitor. To take the love she offered with such abandon and throw it back at her. She would never forgive him. He didn't deserve to be forgiven. "What have I done?"

"What have you done?" she said, sitting up in the bed and pulling the sheet around her. "I'd say we've made love. And quite satisfactorily I might add." She smiled and let out a long, slow sigh. "That was the plan, you see."

"The plan?"

"Oh never mind. What's done is done. I love you, Ryan."

"Don't say it."

"Ryan, I think I—"

"That's just it, you haven't been thinking," he said. He knew he was being cruel, but he couldn't let her drop her armor now. The words almost choked him. "You don't love me. We had sex, wonderful, glorious sex—something I've been wanting to do with you since the first time I saw you."

He turned away to avoid the darkening gaze that cut through him like a dull knife. He listened to every move she made, clenching his fists when she trailed her fingers down his back, grinding his teeth at her soft "Please Ryan, talk to me." He couldn't talk—if he did, he wouldn't be able to send her away. He only hoped that he could live with what was in his heart, certain it had to stay there, unspoken.

"Ryan?"

The room was dark. The rain was falling slowly and steadily now. It isn't going to get better, he thought, ever.

He rubbed at his eyes and ran his fingers through his hair, trying to shake off the feeling that this was a dream. He swung his legs over the edge of the bed and turned on the bedside lamp. He picked up the sweatshirt that had fallen on the floor and tossed it back on the bed.

Like a sleepwalker, he made his way to the dresser,

pulled out a clean pair of jeans, and clumsily pulled them on. Only then did he dare look at her again.

She was slipping the sweatshirt over her head.

He resisted the urge to touch the wisps of hair that curled so sweetly around her face. "Finish getting dressed, Summer. I'll take you back to Aunt Carrie's." He walked quickly out of the bedroom.

Summer broke the silence between them when the Jeep started down the winding drive to Alford Place. "There's something else I wanted to tell you," she said, watching the dripping Spanish moss outside the window.

"You don't have to say anything else, Summer. What happened back there was my fault. I shouldn't have—"

"Stop it!" she said. "Please, at least don't take that away from me." The silence fell again, heavier this time. Summer cleared her throat. "It's about the half-way house," she said as they pulled to a stop in front of Alford's wide porch.

"Humantec has probably taken care of any chance for that little project," he said. His voice had an unpleasant edge to it, as if he wanted her to fight him.

"You're going to get your house," she said evenly. "I'm sure of it."

"The board hasn't made its decision yet, Summer." He opened the car door.

"Wait, hear me out," she said, grabbing his arm. He flinched, but didn't pull away. "Your board would have to be crazy to turn down Humantec's offer."

"What offer?"

She described the plan as enthusiastically as she could under his deadpan stare. When she recounted her call to Max, his jaw tightened.

"So good old Maxwell is going to pull a rabbit out of a hat, is he?" said Ryan. This time he did open the door. Summer got out and hurried around the car to his side.

"He's sure to sell the idea to Roscoe. Sandy Flats is an excellent test site," said Summer.

Ryan leaned against the Jeep. "I must admit, your partner does have a talent for making a sale," he said sarcastically.

Summer bit her lip, but she was determined to make him listen. "Sandy Flats is a small clinic. It's a wonderful microcosm for development. With a little luck, the clinic's computer system might even make money."

"Well now, at least that explains your interest."

"I'm trying to show you I've changed," said Summer, thumping him on the chest. "I understand why the halfway house is so important now."

His eyes remained cold as he started toward the porch.

"Ryan, this will work, I know it will," she said, following him. "I've envisioned additional modules for months. The hospital in Bombay needs this new design and Sandy Flats will be the model."

He kept his poker face, shoving his hands in the pockets of his faded jeans. "Perfect," he said and walked on.

"The clinic will get the full system, plus enhancements, without having to finance the entire load," she said quickly, catching up with him at the porch steps. "You'll be running your halfway house in no time."

"So you've fixed everything." He closed his eyes. "Thank you, Summer. This makes it easier."

"Easier?"

"If the board does go for your plan, and if they see fit to fund the halfway house, then I'll feel better about leaving." He kicked at a peeling wooden step. "But I'm leaving Sandy Flats, either way. I won't be running any halfway houses—ever."

He brushed past her and up the steps, taking two at a time. She stood her ground at the bottom.

"You can't leave now," she said, her voice rising. "The house is your dream. You have to be here."

He turned to face her, the few feet between them an uncrossable chasm. "What do you know about my dreams?" he said. She opened her mouth but he raised his hand before she could say anything.

Then, he spoke slowly, as if he were choosing each word with the utmost care. "I managed to get you to trust me, Summer. It wasn't hard at all—I know all the tricks. I've trained for a long time. And just when you think I understand, when you think I'll be there for you when the going gets rough—poof! I'm somewhere else. It's just a matter of technique." His sigh seemed to be wrenched from the bottom of his gut. "Oh yes, I can play all kinds of games."

She lifted her chin. And she knew what kind of game he was playing now. It was called self-pity. And the only way she knew how to combat that was to light a fire under him. "Ryan, what you did was no worse than what Max does every time he goes into a hospital." She watched him grimace. "Max analyzes the situation and does whatever needs to be done to sell the system. You two have a lot in common."

"Do we?" He took a step down toward her, and she felt the hair on the back of her neck prickle. "I work with human beings, not machines. When I make mistakes, they can't be fixed." He paused and his eyes narrowed. "What exactly do Maxwell Pelion and I have in common?" he asked.

She licked her lips and adjusted the over-long sleeves of her sweatshirt. "You both go wholeheartedly after what you want."

"We do, eh? Tell me something, Summer, just what is Max to you?" He came slowly down the steps and stopped inches away, towering above her.

"He is my business partner," she said, taking a deep breath as her eyes held his. "And we once had a . . . a much closer relationship. It was over a long time ago."

"I see."

"No, you don't." She placed both palms on his chest. "Ryan, I didn't understand the first thing about caring for someone until I came here. I didn't even think I was capable of feeling deeply for another person until I met you. You showed me—"

"Summer—" He touched her shoulders lightly, then dropped his hands and stepped back.

"Roscoe once told me you were gifted," she said, moving closer to him. "I didn't know what he meant then, but I do now. You touch people in a special way, you—"

"Stop it, Summer—that's over now. It's all over."

Roscoe Williams shuffled the papers on his desk. "So you see, the board is willing to accept Humantec's generous offer. But, funding for other projects," he said, nodding to Ryan, "will have to be studied further."

Summer watched Ryan's profile, jaw set, all outward appearances unchanged.

"I am certain that Ms. Prescot's close call will have an impact on their ultimate decision." Roscoe looked down at his cluttered desk and picked up an envelope. He held it between his thumb and forefinger, as if it were something that might bite, and leveled a speculative gaze at Ryan. "What is this, Dr. Jericho?"

Summer's stomach was at her throat. She'd watched him give it to Roscoe just as she'd walked in, and it looked suspiciously like a resignation. Unable to bridge the distance between them, she could only hold her breath and stare at the long white envelope.

She'd already known the board's decision had been favorable. Max had filled her in. He'd also told her that the project at Sandy Flats would go no further until they worked out the details with the hospital in Bombay. She knew she should have been thrilled, it was what she'd planned. But the news depressed her.

She hadn't thought there would be a holdup on the halfway house. If only she could talk to Ryan. He was needed here, now more than ever. Didn't he see that? No, she thought, watching his impassive face.

"Ah, Ms. Keeton, if you will excuse us for a moment, I would like to have a word with Dr. Jericho."

"Of course. Thank you for your time," she said, forcing her gaze back to Roscoe. "I'll keep in touch if you have any questions about the software I've installed."

"Thank you, Ms. Keeton," said Roscoe.

Ryan nodded as she passed him, his face stony.

Summer stopped at the doorway to Ryan's office. She had to talk to him, to try one more time to get him to see reason. Even if he didn't love her, she would never feel differently about him. She couldn't let the man she loved throw away his career, his very life. But she was helpless to stop it.

Opening the door, she stepped in, drawn by the familiar sweet scent of Carrie's blossoms. Walking around the room, she leafed through a magazine here, adjusted a picture there. She ran her hand over the top of the computer she'd installed just a few weeks ago and sat down in front of it.

"Looking for something?"

She wheeled around. Ryan watched her grimly from the doorway, his arms folded across his chest.

"I thought you'd gone," she said, swinging her unbound curls out of her eyes.

"No, not yet." His steady gaze followed her movements with such intensity, it made her uncomfortable.

"I didn't mean to snoop. I was just passing by on my way out and I—"

"You wanted to know how it went with Roscoe."

She nodded.

"He accepted my resignation. I'll be gone by the end of the month."

"But—"

"I've made my decision," he said. Touching her

hair, his gaze turned dreamy and the hard lines of his face relaxed for a moment. He ran his hand down her arm, lingering, sending warmth coursing throughout her body as his lips grazed her forehead. His grip tightened on her wrist, and then, abruptly let go.

"I appreciate what you've done, Summer," he said, his voice tight. "Thank you."

She released the breath she'd been holding. "Is that all?"

"Nothing is going to change my decision, if that's what you mean."

Yes—that's what she meant, and more, so much more. But she was silent as she watched the strained lines return to his handsome features, remembering how carefully she once controlled her own expressions. So this is how it feels from the other side.

She turned away, she had no such control now. "I'm going to New York when I leave here," she said, staring at Phoebe's painting of the swamp, almost seeing the wisps of Spanish moss sway. "Max and I will be going overseas soon." She didn't want to go anywhere. All she wanted was to crawl into the picture and lose herself in the swamp forever.

She could feel Ryan's presence behind her, very close, very still. His breathing was slow and slightly uneven. She turned around. "Oh, Ryan, I—"

He touched his fingers to her lips, and she felt the hot sting of tears fill her eyes. One spilled silently down her cheek. He caught it with a gentle swipe of his thumb.

"Don't," he whispered. "Save your tears for someone else."

"No!" She pushed away and ran.

TEN

Summer fingered the pink bow on her package as she searched for Phoebe's room. Braving the scrubbed white corridors of the hospital would be her last task before leaving Sandy Flats. The specter of the trip to India stretched long and tedious ahead of her, making the hurried bustle of the hospital seem strangely welcoming.

She found Phoebe's room and looked down at the package, trying to steady her trembling hands. There had been so many good-byes today: The clinic staff, Roscoe, Marcus, and dear Carrie.

Turning the present she had bought for Phoebe over and over in her shaky grip, Summer took a deep breath and let the air out slowly. Look ahead, only ahead. One last good-bye to Phoebe and no more looking back. It was the only way she'd be able to make it.

She tapped on Phoebe's door and with a strained voice greeted the small form lying in the bed.

"Oh, Summer, I knew you'd come."

Phoebe looked weaker than she'd expected, her face

pale against the stark white sheet. Summer's heart went out to her. "I brought you something," she said, holding out the package.

Phoebe sat up in her nest of tangled sheets, her eyes round and curious. As the last of the wrapping fell away, she ran her hand along the edge of the polished wood. "It's beautiful," she whispered, opening the box to reveal tubes of watercolors and a neatly tied package of brushes. "Thanks. You didn't have to . . ." She sniffled softly and touched the brushes, not looking up. "Summer. I wanted to tell you. I . . . I'm sorry about what I did, running away and all, especially after you'd been so nice."

Summer took the girl's slender hand. It felt small and fragile in hers.

Phoebe's eyes brimmed with tears. "Ev . . . Everything got so crazy," she said. "I was so mad at Daddy."

"It's going to be all right, honey," said Summer, stroking Phoebe's wispy hair. "You can tell me about it if you'd like."

"Speedy, he started in on me just like Daddy. Telling me what I should do and where I should go. We went to this party and Speedy said we should leave. I was so tired of everybody bossing me," she sobbed.

"I know, I know." Summer sat down on the edge of the bed.

"I had a drink, maybe two. That wasn't so wrong, was it? Daddy does it all the time." She shook her head. "I don't remember much after that. There must've been something in the drinks . . . I don't know. Speedy says I started acting real funny and he got scared. I guess you know the rest.

"Oh, Summer, I didn't mean to . . . to . . ."
Phoebe buried her face against her shoulder and wept.

Summer held her close, rocking back and forth,
thinking how comforted she'd felt when she'd cried so
hard in Ryan's arms. Everyone needs to be held sometimes.

Summer pulled out a tissue and asked hesitantly,
"You weren't trying to . . . kill yourself then?"

Phoebe looked up with red-rimmed eyes, shaking
her head. Summer handed her the tissue. "Have you
told this to anyone else?"

She shrugged, dabbing at her tear-streaked face.
"No. It was so stupid. You're the only one I can talk
to."

"What about Dr. Jericho?" Summer's mind was
racing. He hadn't misjudged Phoebe after all.

Phoebe sat up straighter in the bed. "Dr. Jericho
was here yesterday. I felt terrible. He looked so sad, like
I'd really disappointed him, just like Daddy." Her voice
strengthened as she spoke. Lifting the paintbrushes out
of the box, she began sorting through them. "He asked
me what happened that night. But I didn't want to go
into it. Stupid, huh?"

It was Summer's turn to shrug. She remembered
when she was young. How easy it had been to clam up
nice and tight when the going got rough. It had seemed
like a good idea back then. Only Phoebe had better
options than she'd had. Phoebe had Ryan. Or did. Now
what was she going to do? Go back home to Jimmy?
The thought worried her. "Do you know how much
longer you'll be in the hospital?" she asked.

"Another two or three days. I could really leave
sooner," said Phoebe, "but Dr. Jericho's fixing it so I

don't have to live with Daddy for a little while. At least 'til he calms down." She sighed, her smile wistful. "I'll be going pretty far away. Columbia, I think. But at least I don't have to go home right now. You know, Jericho's a real good guy."

"Is that so?"

Summer's head jerked at the sound of the smooth baritone behind her.

"Dr. Jericho!" Phoebe's eyes lit up.

Summer moved from her seat on the bed, her throat constricting. "How long have you been here?" she asked.

"Just long enough to find out I'm a good guy after all."

Phoebe looked down and blushed.

He hadn't heard, thought Summer. "Phoebe," she said, her voice firm. "Would you be willing to tell Dr. Jericho what you just told me—?"

"But—"

She gave an encouraging nod and watched the girl's shoulders relax.

"What is it?" asked Ryan, his gaze holding Summer's for a fraction of a second. Her stomach twisted. "I'd better be going," she whispered, slipping around him to the door.

"You'll be back, won't you?" Phoebe asked eagerly.

Summer stopped, feeling her heart break for the second time in as many days. "I'm leaving today," she said, taking a slow breath to disguise her shakiness. "I'm afraid I won't be back . . . for a while."

Phoebe's crestfallen expression tightened the knot in Summer's throat. She didn't dare look at Ryan again.

"I'm sorry," she said into the accusing silence. "I'll write. I promise."

Her heels made brisk, businesslike clicks on the tiled floor as she hurried out. She only hoped they were loud enough to cover the sobs that escaped shamelessly as she hurried down the hall.

Ryan cleared his throat. "So, what is it you have to tell me?" he said, sitting down in the chair beside the bed, trying to erase the image of Summer's strained expression from his mind.

Phoebe's eyes were focused on the empty doorway. It was all Ryan could do not to stare at it too.

"You're not going to let her leave, just like that. Are you?"

He opened his mouth to say yes, to give her some kind of reasonable explanation, but nothing came out.

"I need her," said Phoebe in a tiny whisper.

"I know."

Her eyes pleaded silently.

Damn. He stood up and was out the door and down the hall before he could allow himself to consider further.

When the elevator doors hissed closed, he was alone with her. She looked at him wordlessly, eyes glistening. He'd come after her without thinking. How could he explain? He didn't want to see her walk out of his life forever. But it would be worse if he let her depend on him. Eventually she would need him and he wouldn't be there for her. It had happened to him before. He touched her elbow. "Summer, wait."

The elevator buzzed and its doors opened with a sound like released tension. But he felt no release at all.

What could he say? That he loved her but couldn't promise her anything because he was dying inside.

"Phoebe wanted you to stay a little longer," he said lamely as they stepped out. "I can visit with her later."

"Did she tell you?" said Summer quickly. "She didn't try to kill herself. It was all a mistake."

He nodded. He'd figured that one out yesterday. What Phoebe didn't say was as telling as what she did.

"Summer, this isn't just about Phoebe."

"No. It isn't. It's about you. And your sister." Her voice shook. "God, I hate what Alicia has done to you!"

"What do you mean?" he said, shocked at the anger in her tone.

"She's claimed your life, Ryan. Taken it just as surely as she took her own." She clamped her hand over her mouth as if the words had escaped of their own accord.

"No. You don't understand. Alicia needed me. I let her die."

Summer's long, graceful throat made convulsive movements as she backed away from him.

"You're wrong, Summer," was all he could say.

The glass doors of the hospital exit swung back into place with a soft sucking sound. He watched her rush down the steps and across the hospital lawn.

She was on her way up. Her company was going to be a success. And he was fighting like hell just to keep from crumbling to pieces in a backwater swamp. He should let her go. But he knew he couldn't. It seemed desperately important that he follow her, crucial that he make her understand. He hurried on.

She was standing in the shadow of a live oak, half-hidden by the tree trunk she had turned her face against. He pulled her gently around to look at him. "It isn't what Alicia did," he said with quiet firmness. "It's what I've done to myself. I've created my own doubts—my own fears." Her face was inches from his, chin upturned, expectant. Why was she making this so difficult?

"If I'd walked out when I was scared," she said, "I would never have—" Her cheeks flushed.

"What?" he asked, feeling her quiver as he let his hands trail down her arms.

"I would never have fallen in love with you." Her voice caught. ". . . But I did."

"You can't be in love with me."

"I am," she said, with conviction that tore at his heart. "I'm not afraid anymore. I'm not afraid to feel."

He gritted his teeth, making himself keep silent.

"Ryan?"

"Phoebe's waiting for you."

She looked back toward the hospital for a long moment. "Tell her I'll write," she said.

"But—"

"Maybe it's better that she get used to people running out on her."

"Summer, that's not fair."

"No, I don't suppose it is." She walked away from him without looking back.

He stood still, every nerve in his body trying to betray him. "Good-bye, Summer."

Ryan hoisted the string of catfish from his boat. His old habit of wandering the swamp had done nothing to lift the aching heaviness from his chest. No, he was going to have to do a lot more than this. The moon was high overhead as he started up the path toward Alford Place, Swamp Monster close on his heels.

"You got another mess of fish for us, I see," said Marcus as Ryan reached the veranda. Taking the heavy stringer from him, Marcus held it high, appraising the catch. "You had supper, son?"

"No."

"I'll fry up this one here," he said, thumping the largest. "And you stay and eat it."

Aunt Carrie stepped out of the night shadows. "Come on in, Ry boy. I've been expecting you." She smiled, a look of satisfaction in her eyes. She linked her arm through his and hugged him to her as she guided him to the house.

Aunt Carrie chatted happily as they walked inside, and Ryan tried his best to follow her words, but his mind was elsewhere. When they reached the bottom of the stairs, it was Aunt Carrie who paused.

"I'll go help Marcus with those fish," she said, squeezing his arm and vanishing before he could speak.

His gaze wandered up the curving staircase to the balcony. One last time, he told himself.

Monster bounded ahead, familiar with the route. Ryan followed, each step of the climb a silent meditation. Tonight, he felt drawn more strongly than ever. It was the first time he'd come since Summer had left, nearly two weeks ago, and it was the last time he would make this pilgrimage upstairs.

He stood at the doorway now, memories of Alicia and Summer mixing in the moonlight that filtered through the window, bathing the room in ghostly silver. He didn't linger in the hall as he once would have, instead he stepped in, pulled by an unseeable force that Aunt Carrie might have called a spirit. But he knew it for what it was, longing—a longing for peace, for release.

Walking slowly, settling into a deep calm, he made a circuit of the room, opening and closing dark, empty drawers, running his fingers along the smooth top of the dressing table. The image of Alicia, once so strong here, had faded.

He sat on the bed and stared at the floor, imagining the form of his sister lying there. He let out a long sigh, dredged from the bottom of his being as he made himself remember Alicia as she had been as a child. She was laughing in the light that sifted through the cypress leaves, her small, oval face turned up to him. "Alicia," he whispered, "I've come to say good-bye."

Monster sniffed inquiringly at his feet.

"It's all right, boy." He drew in a breath and let it out slowly, scratching the big furry head. His gaze swept the room once more, taking in the warm ivory glow. He thought of Summer the night he'd brought her here, how he'd made himself cross that threshold and stolen those few moments to enjoy the simple, delicate curve of her shoulders, forgetting for an instant where he was, forgetting everything but the woman before him.

Summer. Thoughts of her nibbled at his mind like mice in a mattress. Was she in Bombay? Would she think about one stormy afternoon in the swamp over and over again, the way he did.

He lay back on the bed, his muscles relaxing into its softness. It did feel like a cream puff, he thought, feeling the knots that had settled between his shoulder blades loosen one by one. He would always think of this as Summer's bed now, not Alicia's. He closed his eyes and Summer's image appeared, beautiful, golden, pushing back the shadows that had once threatened to spread from every corner. She was the one with the courage. She'd been afraid, but she'd trusted anyway. She'd trusted him, and she'd trusted herself.

Could he do any less?

Who else would see to the halfway house if he left Sandy Flats? Who would be there for Phoebe when she returned from Columbia? And Joel and the rest? He couldn't turn his back on his dreams—Summer had taught him that much.

Summer rubbed at her eyes and looked around her apartment. Lit only by the dim glow of her computer, it seemed dark and cavernous—much too big and much too empty. She pulled her terry robe closer around her and switched on the desk lamp. Squinting in the unaccustomed brightness, she tried once again to make sense of the notes she'd scribbled on her desk calendar.

With a yellow highlighter, she drew a line through the next six weeks. They'd be leaving for Bombay in two days. Everything was happening much too fast. No matter how many times she struggled to revise her schedule, it wasn't going to work.

She chewed her lip. There was so much programming to do. Rather than thrilling her with its challenge, the task seemed to stretch out before her like a highway with no exits, no rest stops, no diversions—and no way to get back to a certain river that fed her spirit.

She stood up quickly, knowing she couldn't let her

mind take her there—invariably it led to Ryan. It was like drinking poison to think about the past, a seductive, slow-working poison that would destroy her if she sipped too much. But still she thirsted.

Stretching her cramped shoulder muscles, she made her way to the kitchen. What she needed was a snack, anything to keep her mind from straying. She would learn. If she could get through enough days, time would make the images fade. She had to believe that. She had to forget the man who'd made her life full and beautiful, to forget the pain of having it empty again. Was there enough time in the universe for that?

She pulled a bag of cheese puffs from the pantry and munched a handful as she returned to her computer. She had to get Ryan out of her mind, out of her life.

Her hands jerked spasmodically at the high-pitched buzz of the doorbell, sending the bag flying into the computer screen and scattering cheese puffs across her keyboard. Jeez, what a case of nerves, she thought irritably.

"Who is it?" she called, retrieving the bag and tilting the keyboard sideways to empty the cheese puffs back into it. What time was it anyway? Late. "Max?"

"Yeah, it's me. You really ought to get a fax machine, you know."

"Why?" she asked, opening the door.

"To keep me from having to drive halfway across town on a Saturday night," he said, then grinned as he pushed past her and walked into the living room. "My date's in the car so I'll make this quick. I just received the new hospital's layout—figured you'd want time to study it." He spread the papers out across her couch.

"Max, I don't think this will work."

"Sure it will. The hospital's not too spread out. It'll be easy to run the cable across—"

"That's not what I mean." She clutched the bag of cheese puffs against her tightening stomach as she sat down on the edge of the couch.

"Hey, watch it, you don't want to wrinkle the lay-out," said Max, rescuing several papers from beneath her.

"I don't care." She shook her head slowly. It was true. She didn't care at all. Not one tiny bit. God, how could she go on like this? Is wasn't fair, not to her—or to Max. "I'm not going to Bombay," she heard herself say.

Max looked at her blankly for a moment. "You're tired, aren't you? I'm sorry, Summer," he said, sitting down beside her. "I didn't think before I came over." He put his hand on her knee.

It was a natural action. He'd done it many times before. But when Summer looked down, she remembered the dragonfly that had rested there when she'd gone canoeing with Ryan. A hard lump rose in her throat.

"Of course, there's plenty of time to look at this later," Max was saying. "You'll feel different in the—"

"No." Her voice came out a soft croak. "No, I won't," she said again, louder this time.

Max moved his hand. He was rubbing his chin with it now. "Just hold on a minute, Summer." His brown eyes narrowed as he studied her.

"Max—"

"I think I know what this is all about." He let out a

long sigh. "You haven't been the same since that Sandy Flats job."

"You're right." Oh yes, she was different, very different—even Max saw it.

"We should've cleared the air about this right off," he said.

"Yes. We should have." It was as if something had finally jostled itself into place. A sense of conviction flickered on within her, growing stronger with each passing second. She could never return to her old life.

"I'm sorry I didn't tell you about the contract change," said Max, putting his arm around her. "And I promise, on a stack of manuals a mile high, that I will never do anything like that again."

"Max, it isn't—"

"But you did pull it off beautifully. Sandy Flats is going to be a great little development site." He gave her a gentle squeeze. "But right now, we've got even bigger deals to—"

"No, Max," she said, shrugging his arm off. "You don't understand."

"C'mon, Summer, you're not going to stay mad about this forever, are you? Okay, your feelings got hurt. I said I was sorry. I won't do it again. Look, we've got a business to run. You can't start letting your emotions get in the way of—"

"Oh yes I can," she said, springing from the couch. "I can start right now."

Max frowned. "We've been partners a long time. You can't forgive me for one mistake?"

"It wasn't your mistake. It was mine. It's been mine all along."

"You're not making sense, Summer."

"You know what doesn't make sense?" she asked.

Max shook his head, watching her as if she'd lost her mind. Maybe she had. She did feel a little crazy, crazy enough to do something . . . wild. "You can handle Bombay," she said, "I'm going back to Sandy Flats." She popped a cheese puff into her mouth before she could take it back.

"Summer, we already have plane tickets—"

"Take someone else." She felt downright giddy. "It would make for a very interesting date," she said, and tossed another cheese puff up, catching it between her teeth.

"This isn't funny." Max gave her a hard look.

She grinned back at him. "You're right. It's business. So tell me, just when am I supposed to program all of our enhancements if I'm traveling with you? Think about it, Max."

"But—"

"It doesn't make any sense for me to stay on the road when there's so much designing and programming to do." Her voice was calm now, she'd gotten at least some of the giddiness under control. "I'm being quite logical about this, Max. We have to train someone else to install."

"That's an extra salary—"

"So, you can wait an extra year to trade in the Fiat. Barring any unforeseen problems, its finish ought to hold up at least that long."

"You should think about this, Summer." His voice was tight.

"I'm going back to South Carolina," she said firmly. "We have a test site there, and I'm going to use it." It was the only thing she wanted to do. With or without

Ryan, she wanted to be part of a real community. Her days of shuttling from her stark apartment to lonely motel rooms were over. She wanted a life full of people, including all their problems.

"We'll talk about this later," said Max, gathering the papers from the couch. "You've been working a little too hard and you just need some rest."

"Yes. And I know the perfect spot to get it. A beautiful old house overlooking the laziest river in the South."

Summer stood on the dock at Alford Place watching the sunset, not quite believing she was back. It had been so simple. Max was fairly agreeable, once they'd worked out all the details. Although she wasn't quite sure if he'd forgiven her for ruining his date. She smiled, she should have stood her ground from the beginning.

During dinner Carrie had twittered endlessly about the latest happenings in Sandy Flats. The conversation was light and comfortable. Carrie told her Phoebe would be coming home next week, and Joel had joined a swim team. Summer realized she knew quite a few of the people Carrie was gossiping about and it gave her a fledgling sense of belonging. She would know them better in time.

The one person Carrie did not mention was Ryan. And Summer couldn't bring herself to ask. The thought of his tiny cottage downriver, sitting empty and forlorn, made her chest tighten and tears wet the corners of her eyes. She had given herself to Ryan there, wholeheartedly, and it had not been enough. She would do it all over again, just that way, if she had the chance. But that was gone now.

She breathed deeply, letting the powerful fragrance of the garden behind her soothe and repair the ache in her heart. It almost worked, until she detected the faint scent of gardenia. She remembered the first day Carrie had brought her to the magical garden. And Ryan, his handsome face surrounded by white blossoms. That was when she'd been enchanted. And it was a spell that would never be broken, not as long as she lived.

As the twilight darkened, Summer felt the growing weight of her heartbreak. Blinded by the tears that she would never again try to hold back, she walked slowly up the path, barely aware of the bricks beneath her feet, knowing only that for now, the smell of gardenia was a haunting reminder of the love she'd lost.

A strange snuffling beyond the hedge brought her up short. Were there really spirits in Carrie's garden? Either that or she was going mad. She picked up her pace, and the snuffling grew louder and louder and then she thought she could hear the sound of twigs snapping behind her.

"Who's there?" she said, into the darkness. When there was no answer, she turned and fled. Or tried to flee. Two steps into her charge up to the veranda she was stopped by what felt like a huge stone wall. She pitched backward and would surely have cracked her skull on the brick path if the wall had not somehow twisted to the side and broken her fall.

She sprawled on the path, eyes closed, trying to catch her breath. The snuffling was next to her face now. And something licked her ear. She opened one eye. "Swamp Monster!" she grabbed his neck. "Some spirit you are. Scaring me half to death."

And then Ryan was standing over her. He grinned, a boyish, mischievous grin that curled his lip crookedly and sparkled in his eyes.

"We didn't mean to frighten you," he said as Monster nosed happily through her hair.

"I, ah, wasn't expecting anyone to be out here." She sat up and self-consciously smoothed her hair, while Monster assisted by licking at it.

Ryan kept grinning as one brow arched.

She resisted reaching for the hand he offered, and stood up, struggling to gather what was left of her frayed nerves.

"I should have called," he said, touching her chin with his fingertips, instantly halting her efforts to compose herself.

Frozen by his crystal-blue gaze, her wits retreated to some dark hiding place she couldn't hope to find.

"You always keep your chin up, don't you, Summer?"

She blinked and nodded stupidly.

He dropped his hand and smiled, as if that was just the answer he'd been looking for. "Swamp Monster and I heard you were back," he said.

Monster sat on her foot and snorted.

Ryan drew her into his arms, his lips claiming hers, scalding and tender at the same time. He pulled her hard against him, every angle of his body sending messages that fired her senses. Her own body curved hungrily into his embrace. Seeing him now, feeling the strength in his arms close around her, was torture beyond words. His hold tightened, sending her heart thudding against her chest. *I can't take this*, she thought, *oh God, please make him stop.*

And then she felt the tears well. They spilled in large drops that trailed heavily down her face.

"Summer—"

She shook her head, unable to speak. What could she say that she hadn't said already. That she loved him? That wasn't enough, he'd told her as much. He held her away from him, and she knew he was looking at her, expecting an explanation.

"Summer, I know I told you to save your tears for someone else, but—"

"What are you doing here?" she blurted out, keeping her eyes closed and wiping at her face with the backs of her hands. "I thought you were . . . When did you get back?"

He touched his finger to her lips, evaporating her words. "I never left," he said. "You learned to trust, I decided I could too." He ran a hand roughly through his hair and took a long, slow breath. "I had to try."

Monster whined.

"Not now, boy—"

He took her hands gently into his own large, warm ones. "I love you," he said, his intense gaze reaching into her heart, lifting it out and far away.

"Oh, Ryan," she whispered, hardly daring to breathe.

"I'm trusting my deepest instincts now," he said huskily. "And they all say I need you. I was going to go to Atlanta, until I found out you were coming back." He kissed her stunned lips ever so gently. "I love you, Summer Keeton."

He folded her into his arms, and she felt a sense of

belonging, a fulfillment that went bone deep. He needed her. He loved her.

Monster whined again, his tail thumping loudly against her leg.

"All right, boy, I'm getting to that," said Ryan as his feather-light kisses grazed her forehead.

"Summer, marry me."

His quiet, compelling command held her spellbound. She'd always known there was power in that voice, and now it was directed at her with full force. Only Ryan Jericho could make a command sound so soft and so impossible to disobey.

"Summer? Will you?"

She nodded.

She felt rather than heard his soft sigh as he pulled her head against his chest.

"Soon?"

She nodded again, feeling the rhythm of his heart match her own.

"We could work it in after you finish your system enhancements. I don't want Maxwell calling you about them. I promise I'll let you stay on schedule this time."

She giggled.

"What's so funny?"

"And I thought I was the only one who cared about my schedule."

"Aw, hell, forget the damn schedule," he murmured huskily and kissed her with a thoroughness as slow and deep as the swamp current.

♀ ♂ ♀ ♂ ♀ ♂ ♀ ♂ ♀ ♂ ♀ ♂ ♀ ♂ ♀ ♂ ♀

EINSTEIN AND PINK
ARE HAVING A BABY!
IS IT A BOY OR A GIRL?
HOW WILL THE PROUD PARENTS CHOOSE
A NAME?
PLEASE, THEY NEED YOUR HELP!

- You first met Einstein, everybody's favorite artificial intelligence computer, in Ruth Owen's debut novel MELTDOWN, LOVESWEPT #558.

- In SMOOTH OPERATOR, LOVESWEPT #632, Einstein met his match in PINK—a computer who could really blow his fuse!

- But their true love was tested in SORCERER, LOVESWEPT #714, when PINK had to save Einstein from a microchip/intelligence/byte threatening virus.

- Now Einstein and PINK are expecting a baby. The only problem is, they need a name. . . .

Read the Official Rules to find out what you need to do to enter LOVESWEPT'S NAME THE BABY COMPUTER CONTEST.

Now, share in PINK and Einstein's excitement as they await their new arrival, and win a chance to give them the gift that will last a lifetime!

♀ ♂ ♀ ♂ ♀ ♂ ♀ ♂ ♀ ♂ ♀ ♂ ♀ ♂ ♀ ♂ ♀

LOVESWEPT'S "NAME THE BABY COMPUTER" CONTEST

OFFICIAL RULES:

1. *No purchase is necessary.* Enter by printing or typing your name, address, and telephone number at the top of a piece of 8 ½" × 11" plain white paper, if typed, or lined paper, if handwritten. Below your name and address, write the name (and gender) you're suggesting for Einstein's and PINK's baby, and an essay of no more than 100 words explaining what gave you the idea for the suggested name for the baby computer. If you need inspiration, Einstein was first introduced to LOVESWEPT readers in MELTDOWN by Ruth Owen, Einstein met PINK in Ruth Owen's SMOOTH OPERATOR, and their true love was tested in Ruth Owen's SORCERER. Each of these books is readily available in libraries. Once you've completed your entry form, mail your entry to: LOVESWEPT'S "NAME THE BABY COMPUTER" CONTEST, Dept. SS, Bantam Books, 1540 Broadway, New York, NY 10036.

2. PRIZES (3): *First Prize (1):* The name suggested by the First Prize winner will be the name used for Einstein's and PINK's baby in Ruth Owen's next LOVESWEPT novel (scheduled for publication in May 1996). The First Prize winner also will be profiled and pictured in the back of that book as well as in the back of the other May 1996 LOVESWEPTs and will receive autographed copies of each of Ruth Owen's LOVE-SWEPT novels involving Einstein and PINK. (Approximate retail value: $15.00.) *Second Prize (2):* The two Second Prize winners will receive autographed copies of the May 1996 Ruth Owen LOVESWEPT novel which introduces the baby computer and also will be named in the back of that book and the other May 1996 LOVESWEPTs as runners up to the First Prize winner. (Approximate retail value: $4.50.)

3. Contest entries must be postmarked and received by August 1, 1995, and all entrants must be 21 or older on the date of entry. The entries submitted will be judged by Ruth Owen and members of the LOVESWEPT Editorial Staff on the basis of the originality and creativity shown in the choice of a name for the baby computer and the thoughtfulness and writing ability reflected in the accompanying essay. If there are insufficient entries or if, in the judge's sole opinion, no entry contains a suitable name for the baby computer, Bantam reserves the right not to declare a winner for either or both Prizes. If Bantam determines not to award the First Prize, any winners selected for the Second Prize will receive an autographed copy of the May 1996 Ruth Owen LOVESWEPT which introduces the baby computer but will not be named in the back of that book and the other May 1996 LOVESWEPTs. All of the judges' decisions are final and binding. All essays must be original. Entries become the property of Bantam Books and will not be returned. Bantam Books is not responsible for incomplete or lost or misdirected entries.

4. Winners will be notified by mail on or about September 1, 1995. Winners have 14 days from the date of notice in which to accept their prize award or an alternate winner will be chosen. Odds of winning are dependent on the number of entries received. Prizes are non-transferable and no substitutions are allowed. Winners may be required to execute an Affidavit Of Eligibility And Promotional Release supplied by Bantam Books and the First Prize Winner will need to supply a photograph for inclusion in the one-page profile. Entering the Contest constitutes permission for use of the winner's name, address (city and state), photograph, biographical profile, and the name and essay submitted for publicity and promotional purposes, with no additional compensation.

5. Employees of Bantam Books, Bantam Doubleday Dell Publishing Group, Inc., their subsidiaries and affiliates, and their immediate family members are not eligible to enter. This Contest is open to residents of the U.S. and Canada, excluding the Province of Quebec, and is void wherever prohibited or restricted by law. Taxes, if any, are the winner's sole responsibility.

6. The winners of the Contest will be announced in Ruth Owen's May 1996 LOVE-SWEPT novel as well as in other LOVESWEPTs published in May 1996.

THE EDITORS'
CORNER

Be sure to scope out a spot in the shade to share with the four sultry LOVESWEPT romances headed your way next month. This picnic packs a menu of intoxicating love stories spiced with passion and a hint of fate.

USA Today bestselling author Patricia Potter cooks up an intoxicating blend of conflict and emotions in her latest, **IMPETUOUS**, LOVESWEPT #746. Like an exotic gypsy, PR whiz Gillian Collins sweeps into Steven Morrow's office and begins her crusade to win his consent for a splashier grand opening of his latest project! He's always preferred practical, reliable, safe—but Gillian enchants him, makes him hunger for pleasures he's never known. Patricia Potter demonstrates how good it can be when the course of true love doesn't quite run smooth.

Judy Gill offers double doses of love and laughter with **TWICE THE TROUBLE**, LOVESWEPT #747. Maggie Adair is magnificent when riled, John Martin decides with admiration—no lioness could have protected her cub more fiercely! But once Maggie learns that her adopted daughter and his were twins separated at birth, shock turns to longing for this man who can make them a family, a lover who needs her fire. Judy Gill transforms a surprising act of fate into this witty, touching, and tenderly sensual romance.

The moment she sees the desert renegade, Carol Lawson instantly knows Cody Briggs is her **DREAM LOVER**, LOVESWEPT #748, by Adrienne Staff. Seeing the spectacular mesa country through his eyes awakens her senses, makes her yearn to taste forbidden fire on his lips—but when Cody offers to trade his secrets for hers, she runs. Mesmerizing in emotion, searing in sensuality, this spellbinding tale of yearning and heartbreak, ecstasy and betrayal, is Adrienne Staff's most unforgettable novel yet.

With more sizzle than a desert at high noon, Gayle Kasper presents **HERE COMES THE BRIDE**, LOVESWEPT #748. Nick Killian's underwear is as wicked as his grin, Fiona Ames thinks as the silk boxers spill all over the luggage carousel from his open suitcase! She's flown to Las Vegas to talk her father out of marrying Nick's aunt, never expecting to find an ally in the brash divorce lawyer. When the late-night strategy sessions inspire a whirlwind romance, Nick vows it won't last. Can Fiona show him their love is no mirage? Experience Gayle Kasper's special talent for creating delectable characters whose headlong fall into love is guaranteed to astonish and delight.

Happy reading!

With warmest wishes,

Beth de Guzman

Shauna Summers

Beth de Guzman
Senior Editor

Shauna Summers
Associate Editor

P.S. Watch for these spectacular Bantam women's fiction titles slated for July: From *The New York Times* bestselling author Amanda Quick comes her newest hardcover, **MYSTIQUE**, a tantalizing tale of a legendary knight, a headstrong lady, and a daring quest for a mysterious crystal; fast-rising star Jane Feather spins a dazzling tale of espionage in **VIOLET** in which a beautiful bandit accepts a mission more dangerous than she knows; **MOTHER LOVE**, highly acclaimed Judith Henry Wall's provocative new novel, tests the limits of maternal bonds to uncover what happens when a child commits an act that goes against a mother's deepest beliefs; in Pamela Morsi's delightful **HEAVEN SENT**, the preacher's daughter sets out to trap herself a husband and ends up with the local moonshiner and a taste of passion more intoxicating than his corn liquor; Elizabeth Elliott's spectacular debut, **THE WARLORD,** is a magical and captivating tale of a woman who must dare to love the man she fears the most. Check out next month's LOVESWEPTS for a sneak peek at these compelling novels. And immediately following this page, look for a preview of the wonderful romances from Bantam that *are available now!*

Don't miss these extraordinary books
by your favorite Bantam authors

On sale in May:

FAIREST OF THEM ALL
by Teresa Medeiros

TEMPTING MORALITY
by Geralyn Dawson

FAIREST OF THEM ALL

by best-selling author
TERESA MEDEIROS

Teresa Medeiros has skyrocketed into the front ranks of best-selling romance authors following the phenomenal success of THIEF OF HEARTS, WHISPER OF ROSES, and ONCE AN ANGEL. FAIREST OF THEM ALL is her most enchanting romance ever.

She was rumored to be the fairest woman in all of England. But Holly de Chastel considered her beauty a curse. She had turned away scores of suitors with various ruses, both fair and foul. Now she was to be the prize in a tournament of eager knights. Holly had no intention of wedding any of them and concocted a plan to disguise her beauty. Yet she didn't plan on Sir Austyn of Gavenmore. The darkly handsome Welshman was looking for a plain bride and Holly seemed to fit the bill. When he learned that he'd been tricked, it was too late. Sir Austyn was already in love—and under the dark curse of Gavenmore.

Sweeter than the winds of heav'n is my lady's
     breath,
Her voice the melodious cooing of a dove.
Her teeth are snowy steeds,
Her lips sugared rose petals,
That coax from my heart promises of love.

Holly smothered a yawn into her hand as the minstrel strummed his lute and drew breath for another
verse. She feared she'd nod off into her wine before
he got around to praising any attributes below her
neck. Which might be just as well.

A soulful chord vibrated in the air.

The envy of every swan is my lady's graceful
     throat,
Her ears the plush velvet of a rabbit's
Her raven curls a mink's delight.
But far more comely in my sight—

Holly cast the generous swell of her samite-clad
bosom a nervous glance, wondering desperately if
teats rhymed with *rabbit's*.

The minstrel cocked his head and sang, "are the
plump, tempting pillows of her—"

"Holly Felicia Bernadette de Chastel!"

Holly winced as the minstrel's nimble fingers tangled in the lutestrings with a discordant twang. Even
from a distance, her papa's bellow rattled the ewer of
spiced wine on the wooden table. Elspeth, her nurse,
shot her a panicked look before ducking so deep into
the window embrasure that her nose nearly touched
the tapestry she was stitching.

Furious footsteps stampeded up the winding stairs
toward the solar. Holly lifted her goblet in a half-

hearted toast to the paling bard. She'd never grown immune to her father's displeasure. She'd simply learned to hide its effects. As he stormed in, she consoled herself with the knowledge that he was utterly oblivious to the presence of the man reclining on the high-backed bench opposite her.

Bernard de Chastel's ruddy complexion betrayed the Saxon heritage he would have loved to deny. Holly's trepidation grew as she recognized the ducal seal on the wafer of wax being methodically kneaded by his beefy fist.

He waved the damning sheaf of lambskin at her. "Have you any idea what this is, girl?"

She popped a sweetmeat in her mouth and shook her head, blinking innocently. Brother Nathanael, her acerbic tutor, had taught her well. A lady should never speak with her mouth occupied by other than her tongue.

Flicking away the mangled seal with his thumb, her papa snapped open the letter and read, " 'It is with great regret and a laden heart that I must withdraw my suit for your daughter's hand. Although I find her charms unparalleled in my experience' "—he paused for a skeptical snort—" 'I cannot risk exposing my heir to the grave condition Lady Holly described in such vivid and disturbing detail during my last visit to Tewksbury.' " Her father glowered at her. "And just what condition might that be?"

"Webbed feet," she blurted out.

"Webbed feet?" he echoed, as if he couldn't possibly have heard her correctly.

She offered him a pained grin. "I told him the firstborn son of every de Chastel woman was born with webbed feet."

Elspeth gasped in horror. The minstrel frowned

thoughtfully. Holly could imagine him combing his brain for words to rhyme with *duck*. Her father wadded up the missive, flushing scarlet to the roots of his graying hair.

"Now, Papa, are you *that* eager to see me wed?"

"Aye, child, I am. Most girls your age are long wedded and bedded, with two or three babes at the hearth and another on the way. What are you waiting for, Holly? I've given you over a year to choose your mate. Yet you mock my patience just as you mock the blessing of beauty our good Lord gave you."

She rose from the bench, gathering the skirts of her brocaded cotehardie to sweep across the stone floor. "Blessing! 'Tis not a blessing, but a curse!" Contempt thickened her voice. " 'Holly, don't venture out in the sun. You'll taint your complexion.' 'Holly, don't forget your gloves lest you crack a fingernail.' 'Holly, don't laugh too loud. You'll strain your throat.' The men flock to Tewksbury to fawn and scrape over the musical timbre of my voice, yet no one listens to a word I'm saying. They praise the hue of my eyes, but never look *into* them. They see only my alabaster complexion!" She gave a strand of her hair an angry tug only to have it spring back into a flawless curl. "My raven tresses!" Framing her breasts in her hands, she hefted their generous weight. "My plump, tempting—" Remembering too late who she was addressing, she knotted her hands over her gold-linked girdle and inclined her head, blushing furiously.

The duke bowed his head, battling the pained bewilderment that still blamed Felicia for dying and leaving the precocious toddler to his care. Holly had passed directly from enchanting child with dimpled knees and tumbled curls to the willowy grace of a woman grown, suffering none of the gawkiness that so frequently plagued girls in their middle years.

Now she was rumored to be the fairest lady in all of England, all of Normandy, perhaps in all the world.

"I've arranged for a tournament," he said without preamble.

"A tournament?" she said lightly. "And what shall be the prize this time? A kerchief perfumed with my favorite scent? The chance to drink mulled wine from the toe of my shoe? A nightingale's song from my swan-like throat?"

"You. You're to be the prize."

Holly felt the roses in her cheeks wither and die. She gazed down into her father's careworn face, finding its gravity more distressing than anger. She towered over him by several inches, but the mantle of majesty he had worn to shield him from life's arrows since the death of his beloved wife added more than inches to his stature.

"But, Papa, I—"

"Silence!" He seemed to have lost all tolerance for her pleas. "I promised your mother on her deathbed that you would marry and marry you shall. Within the fortnight. If you've a quarrel with my judgment, you may retreat to a nunnery where they will teach you gratitude for the blessings God has bestowed upon you."

His bobbing gait was less sprightly than usual as he left Holly to contemplate the sentence he'd pronounced.

Dire heaviness weighted Holly's heart. *A nunnery.* Forbidding stone walls more unscalable than those that imprisoned her now. Not a retreat, but a dungeon where all of her unspoken dreams of rolling meadows and azure skies would rot to dust.

What are you waiting for, Holly? her papa had asked.

Her gaze was drawn west toward the impenetrable tangle of forest and craggy dark peaks of the Welsh mountains. A fragrant breath of spring swept through her, sharpening her nameless yearning. Genuine tears pricked her eyelids.

"Oh, Elspeth. What *am* I waiting for?"

As Elspeth stroked the crown of her head, Holly longed to sniffle and wail. But she could only cry as she'd been taught, each tear trickling like a flawless diamond down the burnished pearl of her cheek.

TEMPTING
MORALITY
by Geralyn Dawson

"One of the best new authors to come along in years—fresh, charming, and romantic!"*

She was a fraud. That's what Zach Burkett thought when he caught sight of Miss Morality Brown testifying at a town meeting. A deliciously enticing fraud would be the perfect cover for his scheme to pay back the "godly" folk of Cottonwood Creek for their cruel betrayal. But Zach was wrong: far from being a con, the nearly irresistible angel was a genuine innocent. And only after he'd shamelessly tempted her to passion would he discover that he'd endangered his own vengeful heart.

He was the answer to her prayers. That's what Morality Brown thought when she gazed up into Zach Burkett's wicked blue eyes. It hardly mattered that the slow-drawling, smooth-talking rogue was a self-confessed sinner, or that she sensed a hidden purpose behind his charm. In his arms, she found the heaven she'd always longed for. But all too soon, she'd discover the terrible truth about the man who'd stolen her heart. Scarred by the past, he lives for revenge—and it will take a miracle of love to save his soul.

* *New York Times* best-selling author Jill Barnett

Flickering torches cast shadows across the faces of the faithful gathered to hear Reverend J. P. Harrison, founder of the Church of the Word's Healing Faith, preach his message. Anticipation gripped the listeners as the reverend stepped up to the lectern, and the low-pitched murmur of voices died as he sounded out a greeting.

"Brothers and sisters in the Lord!" boomed J. P. Harrison. "I have travelled God's great southland long enough to learn that wherever a few of His children are gathered together, devil doubts and disbelief walk among us." Thick salt-and-pepper eyebrows lowered ominously when he stared into faces as if searching for signs of the devil.

His voice dropped. "Doubting Thomases lurk here even now, maybe sitting next to you." Silence descended on the crowd as individuals shot nervous glances to those seated at their sides.

"But the gospel truth . . ." the reverend's cry rang out. "The gospel truth is that God's work needs the support of Doubting Thomases, too! In a few moments, I'll tell you how each and every one of you assembled here tonight can lend a hand to the Lord's work. Right now, I want you to rejoice with me in God's Miracles."

With an actor's sense of timing, he waited, hands uplifted, for the swell of voices from the crowd to subside. Then he reached into the pulpit and pulled out a stack of newsprint. "*The Petersburg Republican, The Greenville Mountaineer, The Charleston Daily Courier*, all carry word of God's work on their front pages." Waving one of the papers, he roared, "I don't ask you to take my word for God's glory. Trust your own eyes, your own ears. Open your hearts to His greatness working among us."

The reverend pulled a pair of wire spectacles from his vest pocket and hooked them over his ears. Brandishing a news sheet, he read with reverence, " 'Miracle Miss Cured.' " Holding up a second paper, he intoned, " 'Miracle Worked Before Hundreds.' " Tone rising to full bellow, he cried, " 'Reverend Harrison Heals Blind Niece Before Charleston's Elite!' " He held the newspapers aloft while murmurs rippled through the assembly.

Dropping the sheets back onto the pulpit, the reverend spoke in a voice as soft as the night breeze. "But you, my brothers and sisters, *you* don't have to believe these fine newspapers. God's Miracle waits among us here in Cottonwood Creek, Texas, tonight. Open your hearts to proof of God's greatness, straight from one who personally knows His healing. Brothers and sisters, I give you my niece, Miss Morality Brown."

Zach sat up. He blinked his eyes, then looked again. My Lord, the gal could make a cowboy forget his horse.

The gray dress fit her like paper on the wall, displaying the kind of curves that made a man's mouth water. Yet, as bountiful as were her womanly gifts, the young lady who stood before the crowd was the very picture of wide-eyed innocence.

It was a nearly irresistible combination.

"Good evening." She folded her hands demurely and spoke in a strong, sincere voice. "I stand here before you to offer testimony of the miracle the Lord worked through the hands of my uncle, Reverend Harrison."

Zach's mouth lifted in a sardonic grin. Well, who'd have thought it? The gal was a hell of an actress. Lies and miracles, huh?

Everything was a scam.

"I was a young girl when an accident caused me to go blind," she declared. "For years I lived in a world of darkness, able to do little for myself, dependent upon others for the most simple things. I didn't even know my loved ones' faces. It was a sad and lonely existence, despite the efforts of my uncle and his wife, God rest her soul."

Keep tugging those heartstrings, sweet one, and their fingers will reach deeper into pockets.

Miss Brown glanced at him, and Zach lifted a brow at the nervousness she betrayed in that fleeting moment. She continued, "My uncle's work sent us from city to city, and in every one, my aunt would seek out the best doctors to examine my eyes. Time and again we were told to accept my condition as permanent. Following my aunt's untimely death, reality forced me to abandon hope of a cure."

She was good. Zach casually shifted in his seat to get a look at the folks sitting beside him. *Got 'em hooked, honey. Reel 'em in.*

Almost as if she'd heard him, she said, "Then, eight years ago in Charleston, West Virginia, a miracle·happened. The day began as any other. My uncle set up his booth at a fair where he demonstrated the revolutionary new cleaning compound he had invented. I assisted as best I could, working mainly with a cotton cloth he used in the demonstrations. While I wasn't aware of it at the time, my uncle made it a practice to pray every day for my deliverance from affliction."

Pausing, she gifted the crowd with an angelic smile. "That spring morning, the Lord chose to answer his prayers."

Miss Brown reached for a cup atop a table behind

the pulpit, sipped at its contents, then returned it to its place. Zach nodded. Timing was right on the mark.

Her voice rang out on the cool night air. "I was sitting at a table, testing the texture of different squares of cloth and dividing them into stacks for my uncle's use. He visited with the city fathers a short distance away. I heard them conclude their conversation, and my uncle approached our booth." She shrugged her shoulders in an endearing, embarrassed manner and added, "He later told me he observed the mess I'd made of my task and silently asked the Lord to heal me."

Again Zach glanced nonchalantly over his shoulder. Many good folk were perched on the edge of their seats. By the looks of it, this hoax might work as well as any he'd seen during his days on the swindle circuit. He was impressed.

"The moments that followed are burned into my memory," Morality Brown declared with conviction. "I heard my uncle shout, 'God bless Morality.' He touched me, and from his hands, I felt a colossal force. It rocked me, an energy beyond description. Then, I saw a flash of brilliant, overpowering light, and I fainted."

She stopped and surveyed her audience, sincerity shining in round, moss-colored eyes. In a quiet voice filled with wonder and ringing with truth, she said, "And when I awoke, my sight had returned. I could see again."

"And now it's your turn to take part in God's marvelous works," Harrison declared. "Your hands, like mine, can be instruments of the Lord. I want every one of you to put a hand in his pocket or her purse. I want you to pull out the largest bill, the largest coin you have on you. I want your hands joined with mine in God's, to support the healing work the Lord Himself has empowered me to do."

The good people of Cottonwood Creek all but fell over themselves in their rush to add their contributions to the plate. Zach Burkett didn't bother to check the denomination of the coin he tossed in. He sat with his head cocked to one side, his gaze considering Morality Brown and the spectacle hosted by her uncle.

This gal was great, her uncle's show convincing.

How the hell could he use them?

Zach pondered the problem, standing with the others as they lifted their voices in "Just As I Am." Halfway through the first verse, a speculative smile spread across his face like honey on a hot roll. His bass voice boomed, joining the multitude in song.

Zach Burkett had seen the light.

And don't miss these electrifying
romances from Bantam Books,
on sale in June:

From *New York Times* best-selling author
Amanda Quick comes

MYSTIQUE

Amanda Quick "taps into women's
romantic fantasies with a master's touch."
—Janelle Taylor

VIOLET

by best-selling author

Jane Feather

"An author to treasure."
—*Romantic Times*

MOTHER LOVE

by acclaimed author

Judith Henry Wall

"Wall keeps you turning the pages."
—*San Francisco Chronicle Review*

WARLORD

by up-and-coming author

Elizabeth Elliott